The
Deadliest
Game

AN EDWARD MENDEZ, P. I. THRILLER

BOOK 5

Gerard Denza

The Deadliest Game
An Edward Mendez, P. I. Thriller
Book V

This novel is entirely a work of fiction. The names,
characters, and incidents portrayed in it are the work
of the author's imagination. Any resemblance to actual
persons, living or dead, events or locations, is entirely
coincidental.

Cover Art: Book Covers Art

Also available digitally.

BY THE SAME AUTHOR:

Main Characters:

1) Edward Mendez, P. I. – private investigator who finds himself personally involved in terrorist activities that his own family may be the cause of.

2) Yolanda Estravades – Edward's girlfriend and aspiring figure skating champion.

3) Lt. William Donovan – heading the investigation into terrorist activities.

4) Sgt. Tom Rayno – Edward's friend who finds himself on a suicide mission.

5) Ginny Gray – an ace reporter and friend of Edward's who will do almost anything for a scoop.

6) Marlena Lake – a shrewd and resourceful woman who has many contacts in the underworld.

7) Susan Broder – Marlena's intelligent daughter who knows her mother only too well.

8) Louis Octavio – a greedy, cold-blooded killer.

9) Ricardo Montenegro – an unwilling accomplice to terrorist activities.

10) Nella Mendez – Edward's youngest sister who keeps his accounts straight.

11) Victoria Mendez – Edward's beautiful sister.

12) Dottie Mendez – Edward's sister and the last person to see Catrina Mendez alive.

13) Mrs. Mendez – the Mendez family matriarch who reveals her darkest secret.

14) Alexandra Raymond – police court stenographer and investigator.

15) Dr. Claire Ingram – brusque doctor who gives the facts and only the facts.

16) Sam Eisenstein – a diamond cutter with underworld connections.

17) Eileen Kobe – an associate of Louis Octavio who discovers that she is expendable.

18) Professor Moreland – a theorist with a dangerous theory.

19) Mary Riley – the Professor's secretary.

20) Linda Silverman – Catrina's only friend who is as callous and self serving as she.

21) Mrs. Silverman – Linda's mother who is not an invalid.

22) Rachel Schwartz – a bohemian who may know more than she thinks.

23) Officer Morgan Andes – a patrolman in Staten Island.

24) Arthur Corelli – a teenager who asks too many questions for his own good.

Table of Contents

PROLOGUE

LOUIS OCTAVIO took a last puff on his imported cigarette. He flicked the remainder of the cigarette into the kitchen sink and looked around his studio apartment. He didn't like what he saw. The place was too small even for one man and it was dark because very little direct sunlight ever made its way into the room. He kept the apartment clean but not tidy because he couldn't afford a cleaning woman to come in even once a week. His desk had the accumulation of several days of unopened mail, assorted memorandum and notes that were in no particular order. He never paid his bills on time.

It hadn't always been this way. Twenty years ago, Octavio had resided in a penthouse apartment in Sutton Place. He led the so-called "good life" until the stock market crash caught up with him and his ill-advised investments. He hadn't taken his own life like so many of his associates had; but, he had taken severe financial losses. And, it was at that point in his life that the former stock broker's hatred of the world began to take root...and he began to take on other "jobs." These "jobs" paid well, but were sporadic. Octavio splurged these earnings on non-essentials: trips to Europe, expensive clothes and other niceties. He no longer trusted banks and the Stock Exchange, even less, but to put his money under a mattress? Only a peasant would do such a thing. No. The money was better off spent.

Why had financial ruin even happened to him? He just couldn't understand it. His occult brotherhood hadn't protected him from the onslaught of the crash and the cruel hazards of the mundane world. His occult leader, Manuel Mendez, would have protected him had he been alive to do so! Manuel Mendez...that egotistical bastard whom he trusted was dead and the brotherhood was leaderless and scattered throughout the world. Why hadn't Mendez chosen a successor? Surely, someone within the group could have taken over the reins of leadership...perhaps, even Octavio himself or Richard Aster.

Octavio's only solace – and it was a slim one -- was that he was not alone in his misery. His good friend, Ricardo Montenegro, had been reduced to live in little more than a hovel in Staten Island. Montenegro's occupation was that of a public school teacher...insufferable boredom. The two men kept in touch, but not often.

Octavio picked up yesterday's clothes off the floor and tossed them into the hamper in the bathroom that had no bath tub, only a shower stall. He went to put his overcoat on, but first he had to check his leather briefcase: the one with the small lead lined box containing the "doomsday" stone.

He took out the box and opened it. Good. He closed the box and locked it. Finally, fortune was about to smile on him. He placed the box back in the briefcase and let out a most hearty laugh. What fools women could be. Miss Eileen Kobe believed the stone had been stolen right beneath their noses last night. It had, in fact, been stolen by Louis Octavio. And, he was now on his way to a gemstone cutter in the Diamond District of Manhattan. The doomsday stone had to be cut into three pieces to fit into his plans.

He shut the lights in his apartment and stepped into the hallway. He left the building unseen and walked the short distance to the Lexington Ave. subway. He took the train downtown to Grand Central Station. The train was practically empty because it was not even five o'clock in the morning.

Stepping out of the subway, he walked uptown to 47th St. and then crosstown to 5th Ave. It was still dark and the overcast sky framed the city in a blanket of mist; one might call the effect, atmospheric. There were a few people walking to work or rushing into the all night eateries for a quick breakfast or a take-out.

He continued down the north side of 47th St. and glanced at the buildings' addresses. It took only a minute to locate the correct address, but the front door was locked. He rang the buzzer and waited and watched. The front door was reinforced glass so Octavio could at least see into the dark hallway. The lights in the hallway were off but was that the night watchman coming to answer his summons? It was.

The night watchman went to unlock the door. With the exception of Mr. Eisenstein and himself, no one else was in the building.

-Yes, sir? Can I help you?

-You may. I've an appointment with Mr. Eisenstein.

-Come on in. He's upstairs in his office.

The night watchman walked over to the front desk and rang up the gem cutter.

-Man down here to see you. Okay. I'll send him on up.

-Thank you. I know where Mr. Eisenstein's office is. I'll just walk up the one flight of stairs.

-Straight ahead, then turn right. Can't miss it.

Octavio took the stairs two at a time. Yes. He was anxious and didn't want to wait for an elevator that would take him only to the second floor.

Eisenstein's office was the first on the right. Octavio rapped hard on the frosted glass causing it to rattle in its frame. The door was opened and Mr. Eisenstein greeted the man he thought was his friend.

-Good morning, Louis. You want me to cut an unusual stone, no?

-Yes. I am pressed for time.

-Aren't we all?

-Of course. I don't mean to be rude, but may we dispense with the pleasantries?

-We have known each other a long time. The stock market crash still lingers in my mind, as well as yours, I'm sure.

-In a manner of speaking that event is an indirect cause of my being here this morning.

-Here. I am all set up. So, where is this unusual stone?

Octavio opened the leather briefcase and took out the box. He placed it on the table by the gem cutting implements and backed away.

-You may open it.

Mr. Eisenstein hesitated.

-Go on. It's only a stone. Can't hurt you.

A lie.

Mr. Eisenstein opened the box and withdrew the stone: a blue-gray rectangular stone.

-Interesting. I don't recognize it.

-It has no name. It has yet to be classified. Its value goes beyond anything you can imagine. You are to divide it into three equal parts. I will wait outside your office to give you privacy and a minimum amount of distraction., Please, proceed.

Octavio left the gem cutter's office and stepped into the hallway. Yes. He'd hidden his contempt for his "friend." Of course, Mr. Eisenstein wouldn't live much longer once he cut into the stone. In a matter of days, he would succumb to its lethal radiation. What of it? Why should he care for this Jew? He lit a cigarette and waited.

Within half an hour, Mr. Eisenstein opened his office door.

-The job is completed.

-Excellent.

-The stone had an almost brittle quality to it. Its composition was unusual.

-Have you placed the stones back into the case?

-No. Should I have?

-Yes. Do it now, please.

-Why should I? Is it so dangerous? Is it deadly? When I cut into the stone, my fingers felt-

-Strange?

-Yes.

-You're smarter than I gave you credit for, Jew.

-What is that you say?

Octavio took the handgun from the back of his trousers.

-Listen, put those pieces back into the box and lock it. Do it now and you'll live a few more days.

Mr. Eisenstein walked back into his office and did as he was ordered. Octavio closed the office door, but left it slightly ajar to keep an eye on the gem cutter. There was a phone in the office and Eisenstein tried reaching for it. Octavio flung open the door and shot Eisenstein point blank in the back. He collapsed to the floor...dead.

Octavio put the box back into his briefcase. He heard footsteps coming up the stairs.

-Must be that over-the-hill guard.

Octavio stepped to the side of the door and waited. The guard came in and rushed over to the dead man on the floor. Octavio aimed and fired. The guard fell on top of the gem cutter.

Two dead men and the sun hadn't even risen.

December 1, 1948
The Diamond District
Murders

One

EDWARD MENDEZ was taking the IRT train down to his office on Fulton St. and Broadway. He boarded the train at the 23rd St. station and had to stand up. It was the start of the rush hour and the train was crowded. Edward was holding on to one of the leather straps and looking out the window at the black and grimy darkness of the tunnel The window provided a faint reflection of the passengers behind him. No one particularly interesting or even pretty, so he kept staring out the window and shifting his weight from side to side.

The train pulled out of 14th St. when the P. I. noticed him. The man in the overcoat with a leather briefcase on his lap was staring up at him. Edward pretended to be still looking out the window. He didn't recognize this man, but the man recognized Edward as the private detective who brought down the serial killer, Angel Correa.

Neither man acknowledged the other, but Edward cataloged the man's face and general appearance in his shamus' mind. He knew the criminal type when he saw it and wondered what this man's story was and his crime.

Edward got off at Fulton St. and made his way out to the street and to his favorite delicatessen to pick up breakfast: a container of coffee and some scrambled eggs and bacon. The young woman behind the counter gave him a warm greeting and a generous serving. She liked the P. I. He always gave her a tip.

He crossed the street, entered his building and rang for the elevator. His glanced out to the street and noticed the gray van that was parked just outside the building. He thought nothing of it.

The elevator arrived. He stepped in with some fellow tenants and nodded to the new elevator man; an elderly gentleman. Edward hoped that he'd last longer that the previous two.

Once inside his tenth floor office, he sat down to have his breakfast. He hesitated. He turned around to look out the window and down at the street below. That gray van was still parked out front.

The phone rang and he picked it up.

-Edward Mendez.

-Hello, Edward Mendez. Sgt. Tom Rayno here.

Edward reached over for his coffee.

-What's up, Rayno, old boy?

-Heads up on a double homicide in the Diamond District: a gem cutter and a night watchman are headed to the morgue.

-The Diamond District? Isn't that off your beat?

-It is. But, there's something a little weird about this case.

-So you thought of me, you bastard?

Both men had a good laugh. Edward took a bite of his sandwich. Not bad.

-Okay. Give. What's so weird about it?

-Well, there were traces of what they think might be radiation at the scene.

-Radiation? Like in the atom bomb and uranium isotopes? You know, the stuff that kills you.

-Don't really know. But, when the boys arrived at the scene, the top of the dead man's work table was glowing blue.

Edward was about to pick up some bacon and stopped.

-What the hell kind of radiation is that? Could be just harmless phosphorous. The guy did play with stones.

-You are smart, 'cause that's what the medics thought, too. It turns out that one of the tenants in the building had a Geiger counter to test mineral deposits. He heard the commotion downstairs and tested the work table with his machine. Christ! The needle went through the roof, Eddie. They've evacuated the building and set up police barricades. Nobody gets in without radiation gear.

Edward sat back and put his feet up on his desk. For some reason, he thought about that gray van parked outside. He turned around to look out the window, again. The van was just pulling out of its parking space.

-Edward? Eddie, you still there?

-I'm here. I take it you want me to head uptown?

-That was the general hint. Technically, I can't get involved.

-I'm winding up a couple of cases; but, they can wait a couple of hours.

-Good man. Keep me posted.

Edward hung up and finished his coffee. He wrapped the remainder of his sandwich before depositing it in his bottom desk drawer. It was starting to snow outside. He got up, grabbed his Fedora and put on his overcoat. He hadn't taken off his shoulder holster or checked his gun. He did that before he left his girlfriend's apartment that morning.

The P. I. shut off the lights and locked up. This was his way of putting off the paperwork and billing that had piled up on his desk. The last couple of months had been profitable and not in small part to all the media coverage he'd gotten viz-a-viz the Angel Correa case..

In another twenty minutes, he was walking down 47th St. on the exact route that Louis Octavio had taken earlier that morning. There was a large crowd of people milling about the front entrance of an unobtrusive five story building. It was an old brick structure predating the First World War. Police barricades had been put up blocking pedestrian traffic. Automobile traffic was being re-routed and no car was allowed to enter 47th St. between 5th Ave. and 6th Ave.

The crowd's conversation was a mixture of annoyance and intrigue.

-But, who will pay me for my lost time? That is what I want to know.

-The Mayor sure won't. Forget it. Not that cheap-skate.

-I can't see why they go to the trouble of blocking the adjoining buildings. Must be pretty serious.

-It had better be.

-I'll say! My friend, Herb, says two men were killed in that building just this morning. Shot like dogs.

-But, how? I heard it was radiation poisoning. Maybe, we should all run for our lives.

-You get infected with that stuff and that's it. You're dead, for sure.

Edward noticed some newspaper men trying to push their way past the barriers. He recognized one of them: a woman named Virginia Gray: a real rugged, tough-as-nails type. She stood about five foot, two inches, had a stocky build, short sandy hair and a not unattractive face that always had a slash of red lipstick on it. She was forty, but swore she was only twenty-nine which nobody believed. He approached her.

-Hey, Ginny, what gives? Help out your shamus friend.

Miss Gray turned about with a big smile on her face. She recognized the voice.

-Eddie, baby! Give us a hug and I'll tell you what I know...which isn't a helluva' lot, I can tell you!

Edward obliged.

-Okay, handsome, we got two stiffs laid out on the second floor with no sign of a break in.

-What about this radiation?

Ginny wiped the wet snow from her face.

-Now, *that's* the interesting part. I hear tell from a source of mine – and all of my sources are reliable – that some boys from the Feds. are in there right now with their Geiger counters and lead lined overalls poking around. And, the bodies haven't even been taken out yet.

-Why not? Medical Examiner not through with them? What's the hold up?

-That's just it. The Medical Examiner came and went looking real worried. And, then – now, get this – they brought in these lead lined containers...and, not just a couple of them either. So, handsome, what do you make of it?

Edward shook his head, took of his Fedora and shook the snow off of it. He trusted Ginny Gray and decided to level with her. But, before he could open his mouth, the front door of the building was flung open. No one came out, but two police vans pulled up and double parked right in front of the building. The back doors were flung open, but Edward couldn't see inside the van from where he was standing.

And, then, the chaos began.

Three cops came out of the building and pushed the barricades farther back and the protesting crowd along with it. Then, two lead containers resembling coffins were hauled out of the building and into the two vans. The men carrying them wore radiation suits. News cameras flashed and questions were shouted at no one in particular. Ginny's voice was the loudest.

-Are the two murdered men in those containers? What did they die of: bullet wounds or radiation? Talk to me, damn it!

No one answered her.

Another newspaper man joined in.

-What about the radiation? Is the city in danger? Have *we* been infected? You deaf or something?

The back doors of the two vans stayed open and another lead lined container was brought out.

Ginny was the tenacious type and so were the other dozen reporters. They were not to be put off.

-What the hell is in those containers? Radioactive bodies? Is the public in danger? The people have a right to know!

-Any leads on who did this?

Edward noticed an older man stepping out of the front entrance. It was the Chief of Police: Malcolm Webster. He never met the man, but knew of him. He was tough on crime and even tougher with punishment. Mr. Webster addressed the crowd.

-Good morning. What I have to say will be said once and only once, so listen up. I can take no questions from the press at this time. The current situation is considered dire, but under control. We must ask everyone within the confines of 47th St. between 5th Ave. and Ave. of the Americas to evacuate the area immediately with no exceptions.

Ginny interrupted the Chief of Police.

-Then, there *is* radiation?

-Traces of a certain isotope have been found and removed.

-Where did this radiation come from?

-Then, why the damned evacuation?

-Were those two victims infected?

The Chief of Police gave Ginny and the other reporters a dirty look.

-We prefer, madame and gentlemen, to err on the side of caution,.

Another reporter shouted a question.

-Is the National Guard being called in?

The Chief of Police hesitated for a moment.

-No. Police units are being brought in to assist in the evacuation which must begin now. Good day.

A reporter shouted.

-Where are the bodies being taken.

Another reporter shouted.

-Hey, Webster, you running for the hills, man?

The Chief of Police was escorted through the crowd and into his car followed by every reporter present.

The crowd around Edward was breaking up so he made for the downtown subway.

Ginny Gray got back to her office on 44th St. and 8th Ave. It was a cramped cubbyhole set in the corner of the main editorial floor. A "semi-private" office is what Ginny called it that had been earned through hard-bitten and aggressive but honest reporting.

She flung off her coat, took off her ski cap and ignored her fellow workers' inquiries. She had a story to get out for the night edition...and what a story! Not a scoop, mind you, but if she played her cards – and by-line – right it could mean a pay raise and additional recognition as the best reporter on the god-damned paper.

Ginny uncovered her typewriter and put a sheet of paper in the Remington.

-Now, for the headline. Should I aim for panic as long as it's the truth...or just the plain facts of a good-old-fashioned police cover up? Or should I let my darling, fat editor decide who's probably sitting on his fat rump?

Before she could decide, her telephone rang.

-Ginny Gray. Who's this?

-You were in the Diamond District a few minutes ago, I assume, Miss Gray.

-Is that a question or an accusation, pal? And, what of it?

-Those two men are dead.

-Tell me what I don't know. And, you've got one half of one minute; so, let's have it.

-They would have died of radiation poisoning, but unlike any radiation known to man. Many more will die after the first demonstration of power.

-Your half minute is up. Did you bump them off?

-The victims' bodies will be sealed in lead containers and buried as radioactive waste.

-How do you know that?

-Miss Gray? Avoid the subways.

The caller hung up.

Ginny put down the receiver. She chose to ignore the crank, but she cataloged the call in her razor sharp mind.

-Now, for that headline.

Edward got off the subway and headed for his office. The wind was kicking up and the snow was coming down a lot harder. He held on to his Fedora and made a fast path to get out of this damned winter storm.

Once inside his office, he shook the snow from his hat and coat and sat down at his desk. He wanted to finish his breakfast.

-Well, Edward Mendez, now what?

He knew what and needed just a little help. He dialed the phone number. And, then, he reached down to open the bottom desk drawer and took out the half eaten egg sandwich.

-Sgt. Rayno here.

-It's Eddie. Let me brief you on what I know, Tom. It isn't much but it's kind of tantalizing.

Edward filled his friend in on all the details: his own observations and the Ginny Gray info..

-So, you think the government might be involved?

-Looks like it on the surface; but, I'm not ready to put a bet on it. It's still just a guess and maybe not a wild one.

-And, they're shutting down the Diamond District? I'll bet that went over big.

Edward took a bit of his sandwich.

-Mr. Chief of Police didn't win a popularity contest, that I can tell you! But, Tom, I need to get into that building and I'm counting on your help.

-That's a pretty tall order, man. I mean, like, your Waltham is not gonna' stop radiation poisoning. And, if the government's involved, no one's getting anywhere near that place. It's what they call a hot spot.

Edward thought it over for a second and took another bite of his sandwich.

-You're right. You know what? I think I'll do some of what I do best.

-Like what? I thought you were a jack-of-all-trades?

-If I can't get into that "hot spot," I can nose around it. Be talking to you, Tom.

Two

MARLENA LAKE and her daughter, Susan, were in their living room listening to the "All News" channel and not quite believing what they were hearing. Susan was the first to speak.

-Has this ever happened before, mother?

-I'm certain that it hasn't. But, the question is why? And, there must be more to it than mere murder. Finance must be involved in some way. Or, more specifically, diamonds or something related to that gemstone.

-One of the victims was a gem cutter. At least, they were hinting at that.

-I had the same impression, dear. But, why cordon off the entire district? The losses must be in the millions.

-Maybe the murderer is still there and the police are making certain that he doesn't escape.

-It's a possibility; but, I doubt it. If the perpetrator had any sense, he'd be long gone.

-Since when do murderers think like rational people? Edward might know something.

-Dear child, you must have been reading my mind.

Edward was on the phone with his girlfriend. He finally got a hold of her at the ice rink in midtown and told her he would be late getting home and not to worry. She didn't mind because she wanted to get in some extra practice time.

Edward hung up and dialed Ginny Gray.

-Ginny Gray here. Who's this?

-Edward Mendez. Any more info. for me?

-And, hello to you too, handsome. As a matter of fact, I got an anonymous phone call about half an hour ago. Kind of a threat against the city...demonstration of power, that kind of thing. Didn't take it too seriously.

-Threat against who and when and how?

-Didn't say. Wants to keep us in suspense- no wait just a second. He told me not to ride the subways.

-Any specific line?

-No. Just keep clear of the subway system.

-I wouldn't take this too lightly, Ginny. Did the guy sound sane enough?

-He did, come to think of it. A cultured voice with a trace of the European accent to it. I'd say a man in his late thirties or forties...good diction, too.

-You're an ace, baby.

-I am at that. And, now, shamus, any news for *me*?

-What time were the gem cutter and guard bumped off? Had to be early this morning.

-Around five...five thirty..give or take.

-Then, the murderer must have known the gem cutter to okay the guard to let him into the building which must have been locked up. You got his name, Ginny?

-No, but it should be easy enough to trace. I'll get on it.

-Thanks. And, stay in touch.

-I suppose that's your way of saying goodbye.

Edward hung up and dialed Sgt. Rayno; but, he was on call and not expected back until late afternoon. He sat back and decided to wait for Ginny's call. He knew she'd be on it like lightning.

His phone rang.

-Ginny?

-It's I. Samuel Eisenstein. Been in business even before they moved the whole Diamond District from lower Manhattan to its present spot.

-How long ago was that, Ginny?

-About twenty years back. Before my time, even. Why?

-You wouldn't have his old address, would you?

-I believe I do. Not Eisenstein's actual suite number, but the building where most of those gem cutters were holed up.

-Give, baby.

-15 Maiden Lane. Right around the corner from you. How convenient. And, Eddie, I want to know everything...and I do mean everything that you dig up. Don't short change me and you just might make the headlines, again. Ginny will see to it.

Edward put on his overcoat and Fedora and headed out into the diminishing snow storm. Maybe a couple of inches had fallen, but no more...just enough to slip on.

The P. I. entered 15 Maiden Lane and almost collided with an elderly woman who was on her way out.

-Sorry.

-My fault, I'm sure.

Edward took a wild gamble. His P. I. radar sense told him to.

-You wouldn't happen to know a Samuel Eisenstein, would you? His office isn't here anymore-

The elderly woman interrupted him.

-And, hasn't been here for twenty years, I'd say. You know something...

She looked around the narrow but long lobby...a lobby that still had its original art-decor fixtures along with the original marble floor.

-What is it?

-I've seen your photo in the paper. You're Edward Mendez, a private dick. Read all about you and that serial killer, Angel Correa. What you doing here?

-Testing your memory.

-Molly. Molly Logan,.

-Molly, do you know where Eisenstein's old office was?

-As a matter of fact, I do. It's seven floors up in Room 7B. He ain't there no more. We both know that.

-Who's there now, Molly?

-Never liked Mr. Eisenstein. Kept to himself. Never said hello. And, talk about tight fisted! Not so much as a by-your-leave during the holidays.

-What kind of clientele did he have?

-Stuck up like himself. Men in expensive overcoats with no manners...and always coming at odd hours...early in the morning, like.

-Did he ever greet them by name?

-Not in front of the likes of me, he didn't. I guess he was civil enough behind closed doors.

-Who took over his office, Molly.

-A court stenographer's agency run by a Mr. Sebastian Sims. Nice guy. A little on the colorful side, if you get my drift, but nice enough. He took over the office space when Eisenstein vacated.

-And, Mr. Sims is the only one who's occupied that office since?

-It wasn't easy for him, at first, that is. Used to be he was always behind in his rent, but not anymore. You heading on up there?

-You bet. And, you've been a big help.

-Will I be reading about you in the papers, Mr. Mendez?

-You never know, Molly. Be careful walking, it's real slippery out there.

Edward knocked on the door of office 7B, "Sebastian Sim's Reporting Service."

-Do come in. Door's open.

Edward walked in to a neat and fully carpeted office. The carpet was a plush lavender with the walls painted to match. The P. I. faced an empty desk with no one sitting behind it. To his left, there were filing cabinets and another desk in the far corner with deposition piled on top of it. Facing out into the street was a private office. Mr. Sebastian Sims came out of that office to meet his visitor. He was dressed in a well tailored two piece suit with a red carnation in the buttonhole. Mr. Sims was tall and too thin and his hair was too long.

-May I help you?

He extended a limp hand to Edward, but his handshake was firm enough.

-Edward Mendez. Mr. Sims?

-Yes. Oh, pardon my bad manners. Please, have a seat.

-No. Thank you. This won't take but a couple of minutes.

-As you wish.

The P. I. got straight to the point.

-Mr. Sims, you took over this office some twenty years ago from a Mr. Sam Eisenstein.

-Oh...him. A rather nasty little person. Didn't like him at all.

-Neither did Molly Logan.

-Oh, she's rather a dear.

-Nice lady. You won't be too broken up when I tell you that Eisenstein's been murdered.

Mr. Sims leaned against one of his filing cabinets.

-Oh, dear! That is rather a shock. When did this dreadful thing happen?

-Early this morning. Haven't heard about it on the radio?

-No. I haven't turned it on yet. Murdered, you say?

-Uh-huh. Mr. Sims, did you ever have any conversations with Mr. Eisenstein? Did he give you any pointers on the building's staff; anything like that?

-Oh, no. He wouldn't. Mind you, I only spoke with him on one or two occasions...maybe more, but not much. He wanted to know if he could keep some of his tools in my office for a few days until he got settled uptown.

-And, did you?

-I did. And, he never came back for them. Old and rusty things. I ended up throwing them out. He had no listed phone number and he never got back to me. Did I do wrong, Mr. Mendez?

-I don't think so. I wouldn't have kept his stuff in the first place myself.

Stay on his good side, Mendez.

-Did any of his clients ever come around asking for him?

A shadow passed over Sims's face.

-Yes.

The affectation in his voice was gone.

-Who was it? It could be important, Mr. Sims.

-He was a tall man with dark features. The type that looks through you and leaves a cold chill behind. He told me...no...ordered me to let Mr. Eisenstein know that he'd been here. He had on cashmere gloves. I remember that.

-Did he leave his name? He must have.

-He did. And, I know that I wrote it down in my log book...someplace.   I don't remember his name off hand...didn't want to.

Mr. Sims shuddered from head to foot.

-Mr. Sims? You wouldn't still have that log book, would you?

Mr. Sims' good humor returned.

-I'm sure I do. I simply keep everything. I'm a bit of a hoarder.

He turned to face his filing cabinets and walked over to the furthest one tucked into the far corner of the office. He slid out the top drawer and took out a marble bound notebook.

-Now, let me have a look. Here it is! I knew it was a Roman sounding name.

Edward walked over to him.

-May I see it?

-Of course. Third entry down. I just opened up the office so it was one of the first entries.

The P. I. read aloud the name.

-Louis Octavio.

-He didn't give an address or phone number. Does this help you in your inquiry, Mr. Mendez?

-It's a lead, Mr. Sims. And, one that I intend to follow-up on.   Were there any other clients?
-No. Just that Mr. Octavio. Strange that he didn't know about Mr. Eisenstein shifting offices.

Edward was about to light up.

-Do you mind?

-Not at all. I used to smoke, but stopped. Bad for the lungs, I hear.

The snow stopped coming down. Edward made his way back to his office to find his sister there.

-Nella, when did you arrive?

-Just a few minutes ago. I'm sorting through some of the bills.

Edward's sister was sitting at the make-shift desk that he had set up for her. He went over to his own desk and got out the company check book. He handed it to Nella.

-Here you go.

-Oh, good. I'll get started.

-And, don't worry, the balance is healthy enough.

He sat down at his desk and looked over at his youngest sister.

-Nella? Anything on your mind? You look preoccupied.

She looked up and smiled.

-You know me too well. I have a message for you.

-From whom?

-Mother.

He took out a cigarette and lit up.

-She wouldn't tell me what the message was, only that it was more than just urgent.

Edward tossed his cigarette into the ashtray on his desk.

-Our mother, the dramatist.

-She wants to see you today. She won't speak over the phone.

The P. I. exhaled some cigarette smoke.

-I can appreciate that. Mother has some pretty dark secrets in her back pocket.

-To change the subject: your car is fixed and ready for you. Mitch drove it over to the house early this morning. So, you don't have to take the subway on the your way back.

-Amen! Not that I mind riding the subway; but, I prefer driving. Nella? You gonna' be here when I get back?

-I think so. I can see that I have a lot of bookkeeping to do.

-Good. I'm expecting a call from Ginny Gray and it's important.

-The newspaper woman?

-That's the one. And, now, I might as well get going.

-Edward? I think it involves Catrina. Our sister did-n't come down for breakfast – which is not unusual -- and the tray that I left by her door was still untouched when I got ready to come here.

-Did you knock on her door?

-Of course. And, there was no answer. Even Dottie tried, not that she wanted to.

He put out his cigarette and got up to leave.

-We should have put her in a hospice, you know. She probably needs psychiatric care.

Nella put down her pen.

-I'm sure you're right about that. She was never the most stable of people. Always rushing about as if the devil were chasing her. The other night, Dottie swears that she saw Catrina actually leave the house.

Edward was about to put on his Fedora, but his arm stopped in mid-air.

-You're kidding? And no one told me? Did Dottie wait for her to come back?

-She fell asleep on the couch. She was quite angry with herself.

-So am I!

Edward put his Fedora on.

-I'd like to know where the hell she went. Anyway, if Ginny's call comes through or Sgt. Rayno's tell them where to reach me.

Three

EDWARD MADE a circuit around his newly repaired
Ford. Mitch, his repair man, did good work and at a
pretty reasonable rate. He got in and started the motor.

-Good. Purring like a contented kitten. Which reminds me.

He got out of his car and locked up. He had a catnip
treat for Dottie's cat, Stripes. Edward climbed up the
red stoop and let himself into his mother's house.. It was
starting to snow again.

-Anybody home?

He walked into the living room. Dottie was sitting
in one of the two armchairs with Stripes on her lap.

-Well, hello, brother, mine.

Edward planted a kiss on his sister's cheek and
handed Stripes his catnip mouse.

-And, where is mother?

Dottie gave him a conspiratorial smile.

-Toss me a cigarette and I'll tell you.

-I'll give you the rest of the pack if you can tell me what's up with Catrina.

Dottie laughed.

-I guess I'll have to settle for the one cigarette.

Edward flipped her a cigarette and made himself comfortable on the couch.

-I hear you spotted Catrina leaving the house the other night.

Dottie lit her cigarette.

-And, I should have followed the bitch. Why didn't I?

-What direction was she headed?

-Toward 7th Ave., I think.

-Did she have her purse with her?

Dottie thought about this for a second or two.

-No...which is kind of strange; but, she was carrying something...a box...something small.

-Any idea what was in it?

-Not a clue.

Dottie took a drag on her cigarette and Stripes jumped off her lap.

-Has she come out of her room yet?

-No. But, mother's in *her* room waiting for you. I think you know where the inner sanctum is.

Edward nodded and bent over to pet Stripes.

-You bet I do. And, I'd better get this done with.

-Hey, Eddie? Fill me in, will you, when you're done? I'll be waiting with bated breath.

-You bet.

Edward extinguished his cigarette. He walked the length of the narrow hallway and rapped on his mother's bedroom door.

-Come in, Edward.

The P. I. opened the door and was greeted by the subtle fragrance of lavender.

-Please, close the door, Edward, and bring that armchair closer to my bed. There. Now, sit down and make yourself comfortable. And, for heaven's sake, smoke if you like. Your father smoked like a chimney when he was alive.

Edward didn't need much persuasion.

-You look well, Edward. But, I'm sure you want me to get to the point for your being here.

-You have my undivided attention. And, you're looking well but just a little on edge.

-Yes. I am deeply concerned.

-Is it about Catrina? I hear she's been out and about, lately.

-Catrina is involved. It is her errand the other night – of which I was unaware – that has brought you here. She took an object from this house. I can't even conceive of why!

-Let me get you some water.

-Please. It's over there on the bureau.

He brought back the glass of water.

-Thank you.

-Do you want to rest?

She took a sip of the water.

-No. I must tell you. What she took is one of the reasons for my staying in this house for so many years. It is also the reason why Catrina lived in fear of being here and why she left so often and for so long.

-Dottie saw her take something out of the house that looked like a small box.

-Indeed. Dottie should have stopped her. Why didn't she?

-Mother? What exactly is this object?

-It is what is now referred to as a doomsday weapon. It is a blue-green stone that is not a stone at all. Harmless, if you can describe it as such...as long as it remains intact. If tampered with, it could wreak worldwide destruction. It can trigger off explosions similar to the one witnessed at Nagasaki, but far more deadly. I've been guarding it all these years and have lived in fear of someone finding it. Catrina has run from it and I fear that in her unstable frame of mind she has given it to someone.

-Why would she give it away?

-I don't know. To rid herself of any further responsibility in caring for it, perhaps. Or, perhaps, her reasons were monetary. If that is the case, then, I disown her as my daughter.

Edward sat back in his chair and lit another cigarette.

-You and my sister had no right to keep such a weapon. You know that. It should have been turned over to the authorities.

-Your father left it in my care.

-Where did he get it from? Who the hell gave it to him?

-From beings not unlike ourselves: a race that preceded all races.

Edward immediately thought of-

-The Sumerian race?

-More ancient than even that ancient race. He never told me; but, I am well read and informed.

-And, you didn't ask him? I can't believe that. You're holding out on me.

-Edward, speak to Catrina.

-Who were or are these beings or race?

-Settlers, Edward, from another world...a world that passes close to our own once every three thousand years.

The P. I. put out his third cigarette and lit up one more.

-As soon as I'm through with Catrina, I'm going to have to notify the authorities. This goes beyond my scope as an investigator. And, mother just where did you keep this "weapon?"

-In the cellar, behind the washing machine.

-Good God!

Edward went down to the cellar, moved the washing machine from the wall and opened a small, metal door. The tiny vault was empty. He went back upstairs and headed straight to Catrina's bedroom followed by Dottie and Stripes.

-Can you believe it? Our mother turning against the favored daughter? No wonder the world's in such a mess!

Edward didn't answer. He knocked on Catrina's door. No answer. He knocked, again, louder.

-Catrina? It's Edward. Open up.

No response.

-I said: open up, damn it!

-Eddie, kick the god-damn door in or I will.

He did just that.

Catrina's room was empty.

-Eddie, the closet. Maybe-

Empty, except for her many clothes: each garment hung in a plastic garment bag.

Dottie looked under the bed.

-Not there.

She scooped up Stripes.

-I'll be damned, Eddie. Where in God's name is our good-for-nothing bitch of a sister? Well, at least she's alive.

Edward wasn't so sure about that. He took another look around the room. Neat as a pin. Nothing disturbed and not even a speck of dust.

-It's like being in some kind of hospital room. Even the damned bed is made like an army bed – and I ough-ta' know.

-And, no dust! How the hell does she do it? I can't imagine our sister doing *any* kind of housework So, now what?

He filled his sister in on all that had happened that day.

-Eddie, you've gotta' report this. The whole city could be in danger. And, those two witches sitting on it all these years. It's incredible!

-Dottie, after I leave, lock up and keep mother company until Victoria gets home. Where is she, by the way?

-Out shopping. She oughta' be home soon.

-Good. Stay indoors.

-I'll walk out with you to the car.

Outside, it had stopped snowing. Dottie looked up and down the block.

-Nice little sugary coating. Oh! Eddie, I think there's something under your car.

-Like what? Could be a cat trying to keep warm.

-Oh, I hope not. I hate seeing that.

The P. I. walked to the back of his Ford and squatted down to have a look. There was something under his car all right.

-Oh, Christ!

-What is it, Eddie?

-You better have a look. And, you'd better brace yourself.

Dottie almost slipped on the snow hurrying to where her brother was. When she saw what he was staring at, she let out a scream.

-Oh, God! Eddie!

Catrina was stuffed naked under the car. Her lifeless eyes stared back at her brother and sister.

-Your sister was beaten to death, Mendez. Every bone in her body was either broken or fractured and every tooth knocked loose. There are cigar burns on her face and other extremities as well. Massive hemorrhaging in the brain. The life was literally knocked out of her. I'm familiar with her previous history as regards the burns over most of her body. Rather nasty burns at that.

Dr. Claire Ingram finished her preliminary autopsy at just past noon. Edward listened for what it was worth. He had only one question for the good doctor.

-Any sign of radiation in her?

-Radiation, Mendez? No. Not a trace as far as I can tell. Were you expecting any?

-As a matter of fact, I was. Never mind. I'll be on my way. When can I claim the body?

-That's up to the police. You know the procedure. I still have some blood tests to run that may come up with something. You know...the usual protocol. Bit of a bore really; but, every once in a while, surprises do pop up.

-Uh-huh. Well, be seeing you, Dr. Ingram.

-What's the hurry, Mendez? You don't seem too broken up about your sister's rather untimely death.

-Untimely? No. It was long overdue.

Edward got back in his car. The police had dusted, inspected and photographed the interior and exterior. Nothing. Even Mitch, the mechanic, had been brought in and interrogated and released. It was now going on

3:30 P.M. He put in a call to Nella and told her to hold still and wait for him to pick her up. Dottie joined him in the police precinct's small lobby.

-Well?

-Beaten to death.

Brother and sister remained silent for just a moment.

-Dottie, I'll give you a lift home. Do you mind breaking the news to mother?

-I'll do it. You go and pick up Nella. And, for God's sake, Eddie, tell the authorities about you-know-what.

-I've got to.

-And, Eddie...I didn't like Catrina I'm sorry, but there it is.

-Neither did I and I'm going easy.

-Is what mother said...well, she doesn't really know if this stone is... I don't know what I'm trying to say. It's all hearsay, Eddie, right?

-Maybe. But, the circumstantial evidence is pretty damned strong. Let's go.

Nella left a note on Edward's desk stating that she was taking a cab home and that Ginny Gray called and that she might be hard to reach as she was on assignment.

Edward crumpled the note and tossed it into the waste basket. He placed a call to Lt. Donovan who was not his favorite person. He left a message with the desk Sergeant that he, Edward Mendez, was on his way uptown to meet with the Lieutenant. He hadn't taken off his jacket and Fedora and he was starting to overheat.

He left his office and this time headed uptown to pick up Yolanda at the ice rink.

-I'm going to drive you home, baby. It's been one helluva' day and it's not over.

He told her about the events that had ended in Catrina's death.

-Oh, Edward, I'm so sorry. I know she was a difficult person to get along with; but, I'm sure you're grieving her death.

-Murder. Let's call it what it is. And, my dead sister probably created the circumstances of her death.

-From what you know that's probably true. She even deceived her own mother.

-She must have resented our mother and the rest of the family. She probably hated my father most of all.

-Did your sister like anybody?

The P. I. smiled.

-You'll always be my Girl Friday, baby. You have a unique way of looking at things.

-So, you're on your way to have a talk with Lt. Donovan.

It was a statement and not a question.

-And, he doesn't even know it...not yet.

-Be careful with him, Edward. He holds grudges, that man.

-Don't I know it.

After taking Yolanda up to her apartment, Edward continued uptown to the E. 86th St. precinct. The P. I. parked his Ford just a block away. And, in a few minutes, he was sitting in the Interrogation Room on the third floor. He had company. Lt. Donovan had gotten his message and was seated at the head of the table. Sgt. Rayno was to Edward's left and, to the P. I.'s surprise, Ginny Gray was to his right. Also in the room was Miss Raymond with her stenotype machine. Edward took note of the stenographer's lovely figure.

-She really is very pretty in an almost innocent sort of way.

Lt. Donovan started things off. He directed his first statement to Ginny Gray.

-Miss Gray?

-Lieutenant? Looks like I made it here just in time.

-You pushed your way in here, lady.

-Power of the press.

-You know I could just as easily throw you out.

-Don't even think of it. Or...think of the headline I could make out of it? Not that I'd want to of course....but...

Lt. Donovan ignored that dangling statement and continued to address the journalist.

-What's said in this room remains right here. You'll get your scoop – if there is one to get – just give us at least a forty-eight hour head start.

-Deal.

Lt. Donovan addressed Edward.

-Okay, Mendez? Why did you call this meeting? Not because of those two stiffs that were taken out of the Diamond District?

-It involves them.

-How?

Edward took a deep drag on his cigarette. He knew this wasn't going to be easy.

-My sister, Catrina Mendez, was murdered. Probably within the past 36 hours.

Everyone in the room was shocked. Ginny Gray was shocked because she hadn't heard about it before everyone else. She got out her notepad and started jotting down notes.

-Mendez...sorry to hear that, man.

-Thanks, Lieutenant. She had taken a stone – a weapon, if you would – from our house in Brooklyn. This weapon, I've reason to believe, was given to a Mr. Louis Octavio; but, I'm not a hundred percent sure of that. I do know that this Octavio character was a client of the late Mr. Eisenstein who was killed this morning.

Lt. Donovan was listening intently as was everyone else in that room.

-Okay, Mendez, what exactly is this "weapon" and how the hell did it find its way into your home?

Edward took another drag on his nearly spent cigarette.

-My father – and don't ask me how he came by it 'cause I don't know – passed it on to my mother for safe keeping when he died. It's a small, blue-green stone. Left on its own, it's harmless except for some residual radiation.

Lt. Donovan was shaking his head.

-But?

-If it's tampered with, broken up in any way, the radiation is released.

Lt. Donovan pointed his cigarette at Edward.

-And?

-The fragment could be rigged to trigger off an explosion.

-Like dynamite?

-No. More like the H-bomb dropped on Nagasaki and then some.

-Is this fact, Mendez, or just wild speculation? Has this stone even been tested? I can't believe what you're telling me.

-I don't think so. And, I wouldn't like to be the one testing it.

-Wasn't your father some kind of an occultist?

-He was.

Lt. Donovan put out his cigarette.

-Then, why the devil am I even listening to this?

Ginny Gray saw that Edward was about to explode, so she jumped into the conversation.

-Lieutenant, if there's even the slightest chance that Eddie's story here pans out...well, we gotta take it seriously. You just can't ignore something like this.

-And, start a panic, Miss Gray?

Sgt. Rayno joined the fray.

-I think we should listen to Eddie, Lieutenant. There *was* radiation found at the murder site this morning. And, they've cordoned off the entire Diamond District. There had to be a real good reason for that. I hear that some of the tenants are protesting down at City Hall right now.

Lt. Donovan lit another cigarette and thought about it. Miss Gray and his Sergeant were right. They couldn't afford to take any chances.

-You've got a point, Sergeant. You too, Miss Gray.

Edward continued his narrative, taking the tremor out of his voice.

-I've got this theory to put out.

-You've got the floor, Mendez. Make it good.

-And, we're listening, handsome.

-Thanks, Ginny. It's like this: Louis Octavio gets a hold of this stone. He goes to have it cut by an expert diamond cutter, Mr. Eisenstein, into how many pieces I don't know. Octavio bumps off Eisenstein and the guard. The radiation left behind is from the stone pieces. Maybe Eisenstein got sloppy .

Edward took a deep breath and almost smiled.

-I know. How did my sister get in contact with Octavio and who the hell is the bastard and what is he up to now?

Ginny Gray lit up and cut in.

-I might be able to answer that last part. I got this anonymous phone call this morning and there was a pretty potent threat about a demonstration of power. Now, *that* could have been this Octavio character.

Lt. Donovan was tapping his fingers on the table and asked a pretty inane question.

-Was it still snowing outside when you came in, Mendez?

-Starting to, again. Can't make up its damned mind what it wants to do out there.

Lt. Donovan slammed his unopened pack of cigarettes down on the table.

-Okay. You all convinced me. I'll put out the alert. It'll take the rest of the afternoon and most of the night. But, you're right, Miss Gray. We can't take any chances. We can put it under the guise of a city-wide manhunt. Miss Gray? What else did this caller of yours have to say?

-Warned me about traveling on the subway. You might want to start there, Lieutenant.

-No specifics, huh?

Ginny shook her head.

-There never are with these lunatics.

Four

CATRINA'S BEDROOM was now an ordered "mess:" dresser drawers had been emptied, the mattress over-turned and the overstuffed clothes closet emptied of every garment and plastic bag, handbags and hat boxes had been taken out and opened. Her diaries and personal items had been pillaged. Edward finished looking through the last empty handbag.

-I don't get it. Did she even use any of this stuff? Nearly all of it's brand new.

Nella shrugged her shoulders. She was sitting on the edge of Catrina's bed.

-We never even dared ask to borrow anything. Not that I would want to. There's a sameness to everything she owned, have you noticed? The dresses are a similar cut and style, even the handbags and shoes...all in muted colors.

Nella tossed one of the expensive handbags on to the bed.

45

-Everything here must have cost a fortune. Did our father have so much money to leave mother?

-Beats me. But, you've piqued my curiosity. How much is all this stuff worth? What did it cost?

-Oh, Eddie, I have no idea. Must be thousands...maybe more. And, what about her journals? I'm dying to read them. May I? What in the world could she have written?

Edward handed her one.

-It won't take much time. Practically empty. Almost all blank pages except for this trivia about cosmetics and styles.

Nella opened up the journal and just as quickly tossed it on to the bed.

-But, why did she buy so many?

-To fool herself into thinking that one day she'd have something worthwhile to write down.

-Well, if what we're being told is true, wasn't that worth writing down?

Edward shook his head.

-Too dangerous. And, she was probably told not to.

-By mother?

-No. By our father.

-Yes. She would fear him.

-Mother is asleep, Eddie.

Edward was standing in the doorway of his mother's bedroom with his sister, Victoria. His beautiful sister looked tired but relieved.

-I know it's a terrible thing to say; but, I'm relieved. Catrina was a terrible burden and I don't think she had any love in her, not even for mother.

Edward didn't have to be told this. He knew it for an undeniable fact.

-Victoria, I think you mentioned once that Catrina had two close friends.

-Yes. Linda and Rachel. I don't know their last names.

-Would mother know?

-She might, if anyone would. Is it important, Eddie?

The P. I. raised both hands in confusion.

-It might be. Better to err on the side of caution as Lt. Donovan would say...and probably end up making idiots of ourselves...especially me.

-What you're saying is that Lt. Donovan would use you as a scapegoat.

Edward was impressed with his sister.

-And, it wouldn't exactly pain him to do it either.

-Stay right here. Mother has an address book on the night stand by her bed.

Victoria took only a half minute to get the surprisingly thick book. She gave it to Edward.

-Let's have a look.

-Eddie, let's take it into the living room. The light's better there. I'll leave mother's door open just in case she wakes up.

The two of them went into the living room and sat down on the sofa. Edward was already going through the address book before he even sat down. The book was crammed with names and not a single line had been wasted, but there were only a handful of telephone numbers.

-I guess telephones weren't so common back in the day.

Edward stopped flipping through it and went straight to the letter "O."

-I knew it, Victoria. Louis Octavio right here in black and white.

-And, there's his address. The old one is crossed out. He used to live in Sutton Place. That's a very exclusive part of town, you know.

-I know. Whatever he did, he must have been good at it. Here. He's still on the East Side at E. 77th St.

-Eddie? Look up a Mr. Montenegro. Ramon once mentioned him. They knew each other from the Stock Exchange. He belonged to father's lodge.

He flipped back a few pages.

-Here he is: Ricardo Montenegro. He lived over at Sutton Place, too. This gets curiouser and curiouser. These two characters probably knew each other.

Edward got up and went over to the phone.

-I'd better call Donovan with this new information. He'll want to see this address book, too.

-Will you head the investigation, Eddie?

-I doubt it. Donovan will probably go on over to Octavio's apartment which I'm sure he's vacated by now.

-And, you?

-Montenegro's out in Staten Island, right across from the Four Corners Bakery where I've stopped off a few times. I'll head out there first thing tomorrow morning. Maybe even stop off at the bakery. I'd better make that call to Donovan.

Five

LOUIS OCTAVIO sat in the old armchair in Ricardo Montenegro's small and immaculately clean living room. His friend and fellow occult member looked well if just a little tired from the onset of old age.

Montenegro's pension was adequate for his needs and inexpensive luxuries such as a new television set that he hardly ever turned on. He was in his kitchen mixing cocktails for his guest. What did his guest want? For the better part of the day he'd been there reminiscing about life before the Stock Market crash. Why rake through a dead and overrated past? He was stalling for time. But, Montenegro knew what was in the briefcase that never left his friend's side. It was a dangerous thing to carry about.

He served the cocktails cold and strong.

-Drink up. There's plenty more.

-You've always been well stocked, Ricardo. You're a good host.

Montenegro sat down on the love seat opposite his friend.

-Louis, how can I help you?

-Do you tire of my sojourn into the past?

-No. It's good to share a past with someone who was there. But, what is on your mind?

-The stone...no...pieces that are in this briefcase.

Montenegro put down his glass.

-You had the stone cut? My God, but you're a gambler. I heard the reports on the radio. You disposed of Eisenstein and that guard.

-I did. And, I decided not to let the radiation do its work. Don't worry. The pieces are encased in lead. You're safe enough.

-How in the world did you get your hands on it?

-I gave up my irrational and unfounded fear of our dead leader, Manuel Mendez.

-You just walked in to his home and took it? I can't believe that.

-If I knew where it was hidden, I would have. No. The eldest daughter lived in fear of it.

-Do you blame her?

-Let me continue. I hired a woman to make contact with Catrina Mendez at the New York hospital where she was convalescing. Yes. I've kept tabs on that one for some time. Miss Kobe offered to take the stone off her already willing hands at a handsome price. Miss Mendez, who had no scruples, agreed. And, the rest was easy.

Octavio took a sip of his cocktail and continued.

-Miss Mendez took the stone from wherever it was hidden and gave it to us for the agreed upon price. Miss Kobe and I were waiting in the car just down the street from the Mendez house. I drove into Manhattan and the transaction was completed just off the West Side highway. I had already dropped Miss Kobe off prior to the actual exchange of goods...and, then...

-You killed Catrina Mendez. You shouldn't have done that, Louis.

-Still afraid of Manuel Mendez?

-Yes. And, with good cause. His kind pass through the veil of death and see us. I know this.

Octavio continued as if his friend hadn't spoken.

-I beat her to a pulp just to relieve my own frustrations. I placed her body in the trunk and waited for the appropriate time to render my crime public. I must admit that I had help.

-Louis, I don't like it. Isn't the son a private investigator? I've read about him. He won't let this go unpunished.

-Yes. It gave him something to do. Now, I can put my plan into action.

-What are you planning?

-Targets, Ricardo, have been chosen. As I told a newspaper woman this morning, it will be a demonstration of raw power.

-Louis, where did this money come from? It had to be a great deal of money to tempt the Mendez woman.

-It was. Let's just say that I was an intermediary act-ing on behalf of an international corporation...a power-ful corporation.

-I know who you speak of: Romo-Ark. It has to be. When you deal with them, you cross the line of no re-turn.

-You don't want to know the details. Trust me on that.

-How did you dispose of Miss Mendez's body?

-Others did that for me.

Ricardo finished his cocktail.

-And, the payoff? What is the payoff?

-Does eight million sound agreeable to save eight million lives? Or maybe, I'll round it off to ten million.

-And, my part in this? Another cocktail? I need one.

-Later. I'm sending you down to Mexico. The money will be dropped off in a filthy little town just south of the capital city. You'll be waiting for it. The details, we'll work out later tonight. How are you fixed for money?

-I have enough to last me a few months.

-Good. Now, why don't you fix us dinner. I'm quite famished. Haven't eaten all day. You still a good chef?

-I haven't lost my touch. But-

-What is it? Speak up, Ricardo. You still thinking about Manuel Mendez? Forget about him.

-He's dead and decayed to dust...we think. We saw the corpse at his wake, didn't we? Could you forget such a sight? I never will. I wanted to spit in the face of the pompous ass; but, I didn't dare. And, let me not speak of the wife!

-You left out condescending.

-Forgive me! I still live in fear of him. And, do not laugh at me, Louis.

-Manuel Mendez had knowledge and power. He helped us become rich. I almost wish that the bastard were still alive.

-I don't. I'll get dinner ready. Have another cocktail.

Marlena Lake and Susan Broder were relaxing in the newly painted living room. It had taken on an intimate quality, which was helped by the new and more modern furniture.

-Mother? Have you contacted Professor Moreland?

-No. That tight-lipped secretary of his wouldn't let me through. I'll have to go there in person, which is what I prefer.

-We *are* talking about the earth's possible extended orbit?

-Among other things.

-Not about the Diamond District murders? That's what the papers are calling it.

-Why has the entire district been cordoned off? They hint at reasons, but don't give any specifics.

Susan shifted in her chair.

-Do you think Edward might know?

-I've tried to reach him several times; but, I kept getting that sister of his. She's nice enough, but she didn't know when he'd be back and wouldn't say where he had gone.

-When did you plan on seeing Professor Moreland? Tomorrow? May I go with you?

-Of course, dear. You're going to drive me there.

-I meant, may I see the professor, as well?

-Of course you may. But, leave the talking to mother. I might have to pry some information out of him.

-My mother...

Louis Octavio stayed up most of the night planning that morning's events. His host was asleep and that was just as well. His plans for that morning were mass murder: a plan that he did not share with Mr. Ricardo Montenegro...although his host must have had his suspicions. Could he trust his host? Octavio had his doubts.

He walked over to the window that faced out on to the bay. He would have to leave soon while it was still dark. What time was it? He looked at his wristwatch: 3:30 A.M. He had a long way to go and his timetable had to be met. As many people had to be killed as possible.

Ricardo Montenegro walked into the living room. He was dressed and holding a fountain pen.

-I couldn't sleep. Can I get you anything, Louis?

-No. Thank you. I didn't get much sleep myself.

He noticed Louis' fountain pen.

-Have you been writing in your journal? I know that you keep one.

-Only my own musings. Nothing more.

Liar.

-I'll be on my way soon. And, Ricardo, book your flight as soon as possible. After today, it will be dangerous for you to stay here.

-I'll call the airport as soon as it's light outside.

-Why not go to the Port Authority and leave the city by bus? It will throw anyone looking for you off the track.

-No. I have things to attend to here. I'll probably leave the day after tomorrow.

-Suit yourself; but, I'm relying on you.

-I won't disappoint you. So, how many people will be killed?

-Don't concern yourself with that. You still have a conscience and that, my friend, is a pity.

Montenegro went into the kitchen to make some coffee. He glanced out the window and noticed a gray van parked outside.

December 2, 1948

The Subway Tunnel

Six

EDWARD PUT his Fedora back on. He was sitting in his Ford that was parked among several dozen on the ferry to Staten Island. He offered Yolanda a cigarette which she refused.

-Better light up now before we go out on deck. It's pretty windy out there.

-Don't tempt me. I am in training even though I took a day off.

-Which reminds me. Why the sudden change in plans? Didn't you have a practice session scheduled for today?

-I did. But, my coach called me last night and canceled. He said it would do us both good to take a day off. It's just as bad to over train as it is to under train, you know. Does that make sense? If it does, please explain it to me.

Edward laughed.

-It does. Let's go out on deck and get some fresh air. It'll make up for all the fumes I'm inhaling.

-Okay.

Edward had to hold on to his Fedora to keep it from blowing off.

-It's a lot windier out here than I thought. Yolanda, you speak fluent Spanish, right?

She tightened her kerchief about her head.

-Pretty fluent. You need a translator?

-As a matter of fact, I do. We're heading to see a Mr. Ricardo Montenegro who is a former member of my father's lodge.

Yolanda held on to Edward.

-I wish I had known your father. He seems so interesting and...

-Diabolical?

-Yes!

Edward tossed his cigarette into the water.

-And, dangerous.

-So, why are we seeing Mr. Montenegro?

-To informally interrogate him. And, to see if he has any connection with or information about Mr. Louis Octavio.

-And, you're sure Mr. Octavio is the one who killed those two men in the Diamond District?

-I'm betting on it.

-Edward, what about that threatening phone call to Ginny Gray?

-Could have been a prank or something legit. We can't ignore it. We don't dare ignore it.

The two of them were silent for a few moments.

-Yolanda? Have you noticed any gray vans, lately?

-Gray vans? No... I don't think so. Why do you ask?
And, light another cigarette so that I may smell the
smoke.

-You're a character, baby. Here goes.

Edward lit up and blew the smoke in his girlfriend's
face.

-Ricardo? Call me as soon as you can. I'll be staying
at the usual hotel in midtown under an assumed name.
You have the details. I need to know where you are.

-Of course. You better leave now while it's still dark
outside. Don't forget your briefcase.

-Not likely.

Octavio put on his overcoat and hat.

-I'm off, Ricardo. Attend to those things that you
must.

Montenegro practically shoved his friend through
the doorway.

-Off with you and don't worry about me.

-Take care.

Montenegro closed the door and put the safety chain
on. He was putting away the last cup into its holder
when a loud knock on his door startled him.

Who in the world could that be at this hour? He
went to the door still holding the dish cloth in his hand.

-Yes?

No response.

-Who is there? I know someone is there.

Montenegro was about to release the lock to get a
look at who it was by keeping the safety chain in place.

He didn't get the chance. The door was kicked open and two men in black suits came into the room.

-Who are you. What do you want from me?

The two men grabbed him by both arms and propelled him through the doorway and down the stairs. Montenegro tried calling out, but couldn't find his voice. A third man was opening the back door to a gray van.

Montenegro looked about in desperation. Why couldn't he scream?

From across the street came a woman's voice.

-What are you doing to that man? Stop it! Police! *Police*!

Montenegro found his voice.

-Go back inside! Run and lock your door.

He was picked up and thrown into the gray van. The door was slammed shut and one of his abductors stood over him. The other two men went to the front of the van, got in, and drove off.

When Edward and Yolanda drove up, they were met by a crowd of residents anxious to know what had happened to their neighbor, Ricardo Montenegro.

-I'd better find a parking space.

-What's going on, Edward?

-Let's find out.

Edward found a parking space right on the corner. He and Yolanda got out and ran to the crime scene. They were stopped by a police officer.

-Can't go any further, folks. Sorry.

-Edward Mendez, Officer. I'm here on official police business. This crime scene wouldn't involve a Mr. Ricardo Montenegro?

-Bulls-eye. From what precinct are you, pal?

-Manhattan's 86th. Lt. William Donovan's precinct. What happened here?

-Neighbor spotted your Mr. Montenegro being abducted.

Yolanda gasped.

-Oh, my God!

-When?

-Before daybreak. She spotted three men in black suits hauling Montenegro into a gray van.

Edward's blood went cold. Yolanda whispered in his ear.

-Edward, you mentioned something about a gray van on the ferry.

-Officer, I need to get up to Mr. Montenegro's apartment. It's urgent. You can escort us up if you like.

-Okay. My partner can handle the crowd. I've already taken down the woman's name and address. She's down at the station house right now. Let's go on up.

Police Officer, Morgan Andes, led the way up the one flight of stairs and into Ricardo Montenegro's apartment. Edward noted that the hallway was clean and had the faint smell of disinfectant. The stairs weren't carpeted and the floorboards were old and worn.

Officer Andes entered the apartment and beckoned Edward and Yolanda to follow him inside. They were greeted by a big, orange tabby cat.

Officer Andes smiled and went over to pet the big tabby.

-The resident house cat or so I'm told. All the neighbors look after him.

The big cat nuzzled the police officer and, then, jumped off the armchair and beat it upstairs to his owner's apartment.

Edward looked about the room not really knowing what he was looking for. He could see that Montenegro was a clean and methodical man; no dust anywhere and neat and ordered bookcases. He went over to one bookcase and took a look at the titles: mostly philosophy and occult books with a few crime novels thrown in.

The P. I. walked into the kitchen. It was clean and neat like the rest of the place. He opened the cupboard doors above the porcelain sink. The cups had just been washed. He took a look at the drain board next to the sink: two saucers were still wet.

-Mr. Montenegro had company and recently.

He went into the small bedroom and opened up the drawers to Montenegro's "captain's bed." One drawer contained under clothes and nothing more. The middle drawer contained dress shirts, a couple of belts and folded slacks. The far right one held a journal, candles, incense and a small, metal box. Edward took out the box and opened it.

Yolanda who was looking over her his shoulder asked.

-Edward, how much money is in there?

-A couple of grand, I'd say. I guess Mr. Montenegro didn't trust banks. I'm with him on that.

-What about the journal? Let's read it. We have to, you know.

He opened it up and turned to the last page.

-Oh, Edward? Want a peak at the ending?

He smiled and pointed to the date on the upper left hand side of the page.

-It's today's date, baby.

He read aloud:

"Yesterday, an old colleague came to visit and make demands. He's a murderer and wants me to conspire with him. I cannot have blood on my hands. But, how can I stop him? He knows that I cannot take a life...not even his. I must play the game. When he leaves, I will go straight to the police."

Edward flipped through the rest of the journal, but all it contained was Montenegro's everyday routines. He put the journal back in its drawer and slammed it shut.

-He didn't mention his colleague's name.

-It has to be this Louis Octavio, no?

-I'm pretty damn sure it is, baby. I'd like to speak to that woman who witnessed Montenegro's abduction.

Officer Andes was standing in the bedroom doorway. The tall and athletic man knew who Edward Mendez was by reputation. He read about the P. I. in the papers. He admired him and wanted to be transferred to a Manhattan unit. He was working on that.

-I can help you with that. Like I said, she's down at the precinct making an official statement. You can tag along with me. It's not far.

At the St. George precinct house, Edward and Yolanda were introduced to Monica Briggs: a woman in her early forties who still had not quite composed herself. Her emotions were genuine and mostly for her kidnapped neighbor. She didn't mind repeating her story.

-That poor, nice man... Oh, Mr. Mendez, it was awful. I've never seen anything like it before in my life. They just dragged him to that van and threw him in like so much garbage. And, he being such a good neighbor...helping my son with his math and teaching him proper English. He was the one who found Mr. O, the orange tabby, and brought the poor thing to Mrs. Miller who took him in. We all chip in for Mr. O's food and litter. I'm trying not to cry!

Yolanda moved over to put her arm around Mrs. Briggs' shoulder.

-Mrs. Briggs? What did these men look like?

Mrs. Briggs wiped her eyes with the handkerchief that Yolanda offered her.

-They were dressed in black suits and wore black ties...all of them. They reminded me of a bunch of hoods...but different.

-How were they different?

-They walked like military men. I don't think they spoke a single word. Oh! And, they were wearing these strange sunglasses.

-Could you make out their faces, Mrs. Briggs.

-They were pale and thin lipped. They kind of looked alike.

-And, the van? Did you get a license plate number?

-I didn't even think to. I'm so sorry.

-That's all right. You've been helpful. Was there any lettering on the van?

-No. It was clean and shiny like it had just been to the car wash. And, it looked like a recent model. Oh, I wish my son Warren had seen it. He could tell you what year and make it was. But, it did look modern.

-When Mr. Montenegro called out to you, did you go back inside?

-Oh, I did...almost. He sounded so desperate that I wanted to cross the street and help him. But, I was just too scared.

-You did the right thing, Mrs. Briggs. Those men would have probably killed you.

Yolanda looked hard at her boyfriend.

-Edward, don't say that.

-Oh, it's okay, Miss Estravades. I'm sure Mr. Mendez is right. But, why did they do it to such a nice man?

Edward shook his head and lit a cigarette.

-We've got to find that out, Mrs. Briggs. Just one last question.

-Sure.

-Had you ever seen this van before?

-Well, now that you mention it, I have.

-When?

-Twice before, as a matter of fact: yesterday and the day the sun disappeared. Who could forget *that* day.

-And, what about these three men?

-No. I never saw anyone get in or out of the van until this morning. Oh, I hope you find Mr. Montenegro. Such a nice man...

Edward nodded grimly and got up.

-Yes, Mrs. Briggs, I'm sure he was.

Lt. Donovan broke into Louis Octavio's apartment in the company of two police officers and a search warrant.

-Okay, boys, start searching the place. You know your job.

The two officers started pulling out dresser drawers and rifling through them with a surgeon's precision...and, when done, the drawer was removed and the bottom examined and "tapped" to make sure that nothing was hidden underneath. Books were taken off bookshelves one by one, opened and turned upside down. Binders were ripped open, taken apart and tossed to the floor.

Lt. Donovan was going through Octavio's desk drawers. What he found was unpaid bills, advertisements, and some rough sketches of buildings and tunnels: the latter two he pocketed. One more desk drawer to go through. It was filled with stationery that had a Sutton Place address on them.

-Holding on to memories of better days, I guess.

At the bottom of the drawer was a subway map. Donovan took it out and unfolded it. There were pencil marks at the bottom, but he couldn't decipher them.

-Must be some kind of code.

Then, he noticed blue circles drawn around individual subway stops...there were quite a few of them. Lt. Donovan drew a deep breath and stood up.

-Well, boys, almost done?

-Just the one closet and the kitchen.

-Okay, Mike, do what you have to. I'm gonna' make a couple of calls and leave a couple of dimes for Mr. Octavio. Bastard!

-Found something, Chief?

Mike was looking through the clothes closet.

-This character was a real dandy. Closet packed with clothes and good stuff, too. A little out of date, but you could still wear them. Maybe, he's coming back.

Lt. Donovan shook his head.

-Not a chance.

Seven

MARLENA LAKE and Susan Broder were on their way to visit Professor Moreland at his midtown office. Susan was driving down Lexington Ave and getting ready to make the turn off on to 57th St. Marlena asked Susan to borrow her compact.

-Just reach in my purse.

Marlena took out the compact, but didn't open it. She sniffed the air instead.

-What scent do you have on today, Susan? It's quite lovely.

-"Joy."

-And, quite expensive. The turn-off is coming up. What a lovely morning: clear, crisp and cold.

-I'm glad it pleases you, mother. The traffic is really heavy.

-Rush hour spillover.

Marlena opened her daughter's compact, held it at eye level and looked in its mirror. Just as she thought!

They were being followed by a gray van. She knew the full import of this intrusion.

-Susan? Listen and don't ask silly questions. Make a sharp right at the next corner.

-But-

-No "buts," young lady. Then, another sharp right and head crosstown on 59th St. We're being followed.

-By whom? Not the police. And, I never ask silly questions.

-I wish it *were* the police. These people are dangerous and that, my dear, is an understatement.

Marlena opened her handbag and took out her gun. It was loaded and ready to use.

Susan made a sharp right turn on to 58th and pushed down on the accelerator.

-Good girl. Now, at the corner make another right. Hurry!

They were driving along Park Ave. and heading toward 59th.

-Make a left turn at 59th and head crosstown until you reach 5th Ave.

Susan did as she was told, knowing that her mother's instinct for danger was uncanny.

-When we reach 5th Ave., then what?

-Head straight for Professor Moreland's office.

The two women reached 5th Ave.

Marlena held up Susan's compact.

-It's all right. They've gone.

-We lost them?

-I doubt it.

-What was that all about?

-It was a warning.

-A warning against what?

-Interference. And, I have no intention of heeding that warning.

This didn't surprise Susan.

They reached Professor Moreland's. Susan found a parking space a half block away from the building. In a another few minutes, they were standing in front of Mary Riley who remembered all too well Marlena's last visit.

-Miss Lake, you may go in.

-Susan? I won't be long.

Miss Riley and Susan exchanged glances.

Marlena walked into Professor Moreland's office and sat down opposite his desk. She put her handbag on the floor.

-Miss Lake, how may I help you?

It took Marlena a few moments to collect her thoughts. The recent incident had rattled her more than she wanted to admit. What was she being warned against?

-Miss Lake?

-Oh! Forgive me, Professor. I'll come straight to the point. I want you to put my mind at ease regarding the Earth's orbit. I have other things on my mind and this distraction must be settled.

-What about the Earth's orbit, Miss Lake?

-Has it stabilized?

-I can't answer that with one hundred percent certainty. The Earth's orbit may drift further away from its original elliptical orbit, but...

-Go on. Finish what you were saying, Professor.

-It is in correction.

-You don't sound too sure about that.

-In my opinion, Miss Lake, we've nothing to worry about. The planet has nearly settled in, so to speak.

-But, the Earth is moving in a vacuum. If its orbit was shifted by the sun's disappearance last year, what's to slow it down much less stop it?

Professor Moreland looked at this astute, if somewhat arrogant visitor.

-Gravity, Miss Lake. Not the Earth's gravity, of course – although that may also play a key part, but the sun's gravitational pull balanced by the moon and the Earth's neighboring planets.

-Interesting and rather complex, I dare say.

-Miss Lake, put your mind at ease. The Earth's orbit was shifted by a fraction. It's sturdier and more resilient than you might think.

-And, now Professor for my next question. What do you know of these gray vans?

Professor Moreland picked up a pencil and pointed it at Marlena.

-What do *you* know about them? I won't pretend that I don't know what you're talking about.

-Good. We speak the same language.

-You look upset, Miss Lake. Have you been followed? If you have, you should be upset. I would be.

Marlena was beginning to like this Professor Moreland.

-Yes. On my way here, I spotted one of them tailing us. I don't flatter myself that we dodged it. It let us go. It was a warning. I'm certain of it.

-Are you in possession of knowledge, Miss Lake, that you shouldn't be?

Marlena couldn't help but look away.

-I am in possession of a great deal and variety of knowledge. Professor?

-Yes, Miss Lake?

-Are you up on your current events?

-I listen to the morning news. Are you referring to the Diamond District murders?

She smiled and pointed her finger at him.

-We *do* speak the same language.

-The entire area was cordoned off...or would "quarantined" be a better word, Miss Lake?

-Far better and more accurate.

Marlena and Professor Moreland were startled by a woman's scream. It was Mary Riley. Before either one of them could react, they heard footsteps coming down the hallway. Susan burst into the office.

-Mother! Professor Moreland! I'm so sorry to just barge in like this. It was just came over the radio.

-What in the world is it, Susan.

-An explosion in the subway tunnel on the BMT line in Brooklyn. It said-

Susan tried catching her breath.

-It said the explosion took place on the Manhattan bound LL train.

Professor Moreland stood up.

-Miss Broder, were there any survivors? Please, say there were, girl!

Eight

LOUIS OCTAVIO was struggling to control his fear and his nerve. He had a job to do that morning. He turned up his coat collar to keep out the brisk, December wind. He was headed uptown to 14th St. to catch the LL train that would take him to the last stop in Brooklyn. It was just past five-thirty and there were only a few commuters keeping him company.

When Octavio reached 14th St., the train was in the station and about to pull out. He made a run for it and got inside just as the doors closed.

-You just made it, man.

This startled Octavio.

-I did at that.

He didn't want to be unsociable and call attention to himself. Not now. The risk was too great.

The train pulled out of the station.

-You got the crown jewels in there?

-Not quite, young man. Just some legal papers.

-You an insurance salesman or something?

-No. A stock broker.

-How come you heading into Brooklyn?

This young upstart was asking too many questions. Octavio reversed the role playing.

-On your way to school, young man?

-Yes. I was staying at my uncle's place in the city; but, I live in Canarsie. It's the last stop on this heap.

Octavio was not pleased with this bit of news. The young man continued.

-I get off at Myrtle and Wyckoff for school. I got plenty of time to kill.

Octavio started breathing again.

-What about you, man? I answered your question.

-I'm seeing some clients on business. The telephone would not be sufficient to conduct business as papers need to be signed. Does that satisfy your curiosity?

He would have shot the young teenager had there not been other commuters riding in the subway car.

-You talk real refined and with an accent. You from Europe or something?

Was there no end to these questions?

-I am originally from Spain, but have emigrated to this country. And that, young man, will conclude this interrogation. Good day.

Octavio moved to the other end of the subway car much annoyed at the encounter.

-That young hooligan will be getting off at my transfer point...and good riddance to him! He's looking over at me. Bastard! It's a damned good thing he's not going home to Canarsie. He'd want to know why I was getting off the train with him.

The train rattled on into Brooklyn passing through the tunnel that connected the two boroughs. It passed one local stop after another, but Octavio took little notice.

The teenager got off at Myrtle and Wyckoff and gave Octavio one last look. The LL heading into Manhattan pulled in on the opposite track. He saw the boy saying something to a heavy-set woman who'd just gotten off that train. The woman looked over at Octavio just as the doors slid closed..

Within half an hour, he arrived at the last stop in Canarsie. Octavio found an empty bench on the platform outside and opened his briefcase. The small lead box was strapped in and there was a timer in that box set for 7:45 A.M. For a moment, he suffered a spasm of paranoia: would the timer work...was the piece securely in place?

He couldn't unwrap the box and check. No. He had to calm himself and attempt to be rational. He crossed over to the other side of the station to catch the train going back into Manhattan. The train was already there. Octavio got on and waited for it to pull out. He found himself a window seat and pretended to be looking through his briefcase. He didn't have much time...less than half an hour to the transfer point at Myrtle and Wyckoff. Once there, the train would be crowded with morning commuters.

He took out the box and hid it behind the briefcase on his lap. He put the briefcase on the floor along with the box containing the piece of stone. He pushed the box under the seat and against the car's wall. The train pulled out of the Canarsie station.

Octavio put his briefcase back on his lap. He looked out the train window, but nothing registered in his brain. As the train passed each stop more commuters got on and it was now getting close to standing room only. He picked up his briefcase and got ready to leave.

After what seemed like an interminable length, the train pulled into Myrtle and Wyckoff. Octavio got off and hurried up the stairs.

As Louis Octavio left the crowded subway car, other commuters pushed their way in. A young, pregnant woman looked around for a seat, but couldn't find any. Anna King knew that she shouldn't have gone to work that day. As a matter of fact, she should have taken her maternity leave a month ago; but, she needed the money because her husband, a factory worker, had just been laid off. Anna held on to the steel pole and made up her mind that today would be her last day on the job.

Walter Patterson boarded that same subway car. He started his new job at the same life insurance firm that Dottie Mendez had worked for, just three months ago. And, like his predecessor, he hated it, his co-workers and his supervisor. Walter was young and just out of high school. He couldn't afford to go to college and his parents were constantly on his back to find work. Hell at home and hell at the work place. If this was the real world, he'd take the first rocket ship off.

A tall and handsome young man was hanging on to a leather strap and staring intently at the pretty blonde sitting in the seat that Louis Octavio just vacated. The handsome man's overcoat hid his erection.

Two nuns were sitting close to the pretty blonde discussing the coming holidays. One of the nuns had been in the Dominican order for many years and loved her job as a science teacher in an all girls high school. She was training the young novice sitting next to her. The young novice was afraid of crowds and sat close to her superior.

A middle-aged woman convinced a middle-aged man to give up his seat to her. Once seated, she lacked the good manners to thank the man.

A young, black woman was worried about the time. She didn't want to be late for work and ruin her perfect attendance record. Connie Madison worked in the Garment District and liked her job as floor walker. It gave her a sense of security and belonging. She was well liked.

Lynette Mason was a receptionist in a prestigious law firm in midtown. She was a pretty and friendly brunette who was putting her kid brother through law school. And, just maybe she could help get him a job with her firm. Right now, she was trying to read the latest best-selling romance novel standing up.

The death train picked up more passengers until it reached its final stop in Brooklyn which was Bedford

Ave.. The two transit cops on the platform discouraged waiting commuters from getting on an already too crowded train.

The train pulled out of the station. The next stop would have been First Ave. in Manhattan. As the train approached the mid-point of the tunnel, the ring of an alarm clock was heard. It was barely perceptible, but the pretty blonde sitting sitting nearest to the box beneath her seat, heard it and wondered what it was. At the same moment, she felt the air pressure give the familiar pop in her ears.

The man sitting next to the pretty blonde felt the pressure, too. And, like his subway companion, he thought he heard an alarm clock go off. It was too late to do anything. The doomsday stone exploded and in an instantaneous flash the commuters in that subway car were cremated. The explosion gutted the car as the chain reaction reached the adjoining cars. The motor man lost control of the train. It derailed and skidded into the tunnel wall causing sparks to fly everywhere. He was flung through the window and on to the tracks where he was run over. Every passenger was killed by the blast or crushed against the sides of the train.

What was left of the train came to rest between the tunnel wall and the subway tracks. It nearly fell on its side as it came to rest at a forty-five degree angle. The explosion caused fractures in the subway tunnel which threatened to crack it open and flood the system. No one aboard the LL train survived.

The Deadliest Game

The radiation was spreading through the tunnel. It reached First Ave. and, then, Bedford Ave. People started screaming in pain and running toward the stair-wells. Their flesh was starting to burn and blister. Some were dropping to the floor blinded and dying from the fall-out. Others managed to get to the street, but even for them, it was too late.

Nine

GINNY GRAY was the first reporters on the scene. She got as far as the First Ave. station with her photographer, Fred; but, they couldn't get past the battalion of police officers and paramedics. Strong radiation levels were detected and every paramedic, officer and explosives expert had to be suited up in radiation gear. There was little hope of finding any survivors. Those people who'd been felled by radiation on the subway platforms were being taken to the local hospitals and quarantined. They weren't expected to live. Those commuters who had gotten on to the street had to be rounded up and brought in for treatment if it wasn't already too late.

Ginny Gray was arguing with the officer in charge.

-Ginny Gray. Press. I have to get in there.

-No way, lady. The whole tunnel is filled with radiation.

-But, we've all been exposed. So, what's the point of holding back?

The police officer looked at this wild-eyed woman and held his temper.

-Where we're standing is safe enough.

-What the hell does that mean?

-I overheard some of the big boys say that there's this sharp drop off in radiation. It's been dropping off little by little.

-You mean it goes just so far and no further and then starts to drop off?

-That's just about the gist of it, lady, but don't quote me on that.

That's exactly what Ginny Gray was planning to do.

-Can me and my photographer borrow some of that radiation gear. Look! There's some right over there and nobody's using it.

-Go and ask my commanding officer over there.

-I will. Come on, Fred.

Ginny was given a gruff greeting by Lt. Dunlap. But, to the reporter's amazement, she was given leave to use the radiation suits and proceed into the tunnel along with some other police officers.

-It's well lit so you oughta' get some good shots there, Fred.

Lt. Dunlap had to warn them.

-Miss Gray? Don't stay too long, it ain't healthy. The radiation has gone down, but the Geiger readings are still active.

Ginny and Fred jumped off the platform and on to the subway tracks just as another reporter who sneaked by Lt. Dunlap was about to get into a radiation suit.

-I'll take that, please, that's mine.

-What the hell- Ginny, old girl! It's mine. I got here first so fuck off.

This rival reporter got into the suit as a couple of paramedics coming out of the tunnel pushed past them carrying body bags.

-Oh, hell! Fred, grab those two suits over there. This bastard can just have his damned suit. We'll catch up.

Ginny Gray and Fred Marconi suited up and followed their rival reporter into the subway tunnel. It was well lit with torch lights and flares. Paramedics and police officers who were all in radiation gear went past them carrying black body bags...even hard-bitten Ginny was affected.

After what seemed like an eternity of dodging cops and medics and avoiding the third rail, the two journalists and photographer sighted the train wreck. The train or what was left of it was at a dangerously steep angle with the lead car still intact but with its windows blown out. Barricades were set up and Ginny and company were not allowed past this.

An officer approached them holding up both arms.

-Sorry folks. Even we can't get much beyond this point...at least not for long. The radiation level goes off the damned Geiger counters. But, you're safe enough here.

-Fred, take as many photographs as you can and try and get as many different angles. Get to it. This nice officer is probably right. I don't think any of us should hang around here too long. We must be pretty close to the center of the blast and that's bound to be still radio-active.

The officer in charge agreed.

-Sister, you can say that, again.

Ginny addressed the handsome police officer. She could see that he was good looking even behind the radiation mask.

-Let me get this straight: this radiation-

-They think it's some kind of new type of radiation.

-Let's just call it radiation for now. It's too intense to get near the detonation spot but drops off and keeps dropping off in intensity by the minute. Is that a fair enough statement?

-It's as good as any I've been hearing.

-When did this happen?

-About 8 A.M., give or take.

-Are there any survivors?

-No. The ones who took it on the chin first were the lucky ones.

"An explosion in the BMT subway tunnel occurred at approximately 8 A.M. on the LL line. The explosion took place aboard a Manhattan bound train at the mid-point of the connecting tunnel between Brooklyn and Manhattan. The cause of the explosion is not yet known, but a terrorist act has not been ruled out. We have no word yet of any survivors."

Susan caught her breath. Mary stifled a cry.

"Reports of radiation have been confirmed. Sources say that this radiation reached as far as the First Ave.

and Bedford Ave. stations. Commuters on these platforms have been taken to the local hospitals and quarantined. The Mayor is on the scene and the Governor has been informed of the situation. The LL line has been shut down and commuters are asked to seek alternative routes."

Marlena was the first to speak.

-Radiation, again. The incident in the Diamond District yesterday was only the tip of the iceberg. Susan? Let's head on over to Edward's office. I must know what's going on.

Susan knew better than to argue with her mother. She looked over at Mary Riley.

-Miss Riley, will you be all right?

She didn't answer, but Professor Moreland did.

-I'll look after her. Thank you.

He turned to Marlena.

-Miss Lake? If you find out anything about this radiation, please let me know. I'm as curious as you.

-Of course. Susan? Let's go.

Edward and Yolanda were driving up Nassau St when the news bulletin came on the radio. Edward pulled the Ford over to the curb and the two of them listened to the radio announcer.

-Edward?

-I'm here, baby.

-What do you make of it? It's pretty frightening.

-I'll say!

-Do you think that this man, Octavio, is behind it? I'll bet that he is.

-You're reading my mind. Let's head on up to my office. I've got some phone calls to make. And, then, we'll make a "b" line to the 86th St. precinct. Things are probably hopping up there by now.

He pulled out of his double parked space and drove the few blocks to his office. When they arrived, Nella was at her make-shift desk and glued to the radio.

-We already heard the news, Nella.

She turned off the radio.

-It's on all the channels, Edward. Oh! Hello, Yolanda. It's horrible! Edward, they don't think there are any survivors.

-Yolanda, sit down, baby. Nella? If you brought any coffee with you, we could sure use a cup.

Nella had a thermos filled with hot coffee.

-Oh, my hands are shaking.

Yolanda went over to her.

-Let me help you pour, Nella.

Edward was dialing the 86th St. precinct.

-Lt. Donovan, please. Edward Mendez calling.

-He just got in, Mr. Mendez. Can you hold?

-You bet.

Lt. Donovan got on the line.

-Mendez? You've heard about the tunnel explosion.

-Just a few minutes ago on the car radio. It's on every call station.

-You got any news for me on Montenegro?

-I'll say! I think I should come on up.

Gerard Denza

-Do that. I've got some news myself. And, the rumor is that the Mayor is about to shut down the entire transit system.

Ten

LOUIS OCTAVIO got off the subway at Chambers St. He had to meet his associate, Eileen Kobe, at her apartment on Gold St. He was sweating. His undershirt and dress shirt were soaked through. He'd caught a chill. His forehead was dripping sweat and he had to take off his hat...that was when he caught the chill.

He was about to cross Nassau St. when a '47 Ford drove past. He caught sight of the driver and recognized him as the man he saw on the train yesterday morning: Edward Mendez. Had Mendez spotted him? What of it? Octavio thought nothing more of it, but Edward Mendez *had* spotted Octavio standing at the corner.

Octavio crossed over to Gold St. Before going into Miss Kobe's apartment building, he placed a call to Ginny Gray. The reporter wasn't at her desk. She was out on assignment.

-Of course. Thank you. No. No message.

He hung up.

Octavio rang Eileen Kobe's doorbell. She buzzed him in. He didn't take the self service elevator that the modern building offered its tenants and their visitors. Instead, he sprinted up the two flights of stairs with his briefcase in hand. Miss Kobe was waiting for him in her doorway.

-Get in, quickly. I've been listening to the radio bulletins. I can't believe what I'm hearing.

-Bully for you. Here. Take my hat, if you would. I'm sweating like the proverbial pig.

Once inside, Octavio flung off his overcoat and sat down in an armchair by the radiator. His trembling hands were like ice.

-Get me a drink. Scotch, straight.

-Tell me what happened.

She was about to sit down on the sofa.

-A drink, please. Must I ask a third time?

Miss Kobe picked up his overcoat from the floor. She went over to the drinks table and got her guest a Scotch, straight.

-Here.

She sat down and faced Octavio.

-You look terrible. And, you're shaking from head to foot. Are you coming down with the flu?

-I do not feel at all well.

-Well, if I just murdered a few hundred people, I wouldn't feel too good either. I won't be a party to this. Do you hear me, Louis? You've just committed a crime of mass genocide. They'll be coming after you. Do you hear what I'm telling you?

-I'm well within earshot.

-You lied to me. The stone hadn't been stolen at all. You were the one who took it. You played me for a fool.

-A harmless but necessary subterfuge.

A look of terror came over the woman's face.

-It's not here is it? It's not in that briefcase, is it...or what's left of it?

Octavio finished his drink.

-Yes. It is.

-Sealed in a lead container, of course.

-Yes.

-But? Why are you hesitating? Tell me, Louis.

-Ordinary lead, I fear, may only shield its radiation for a limited time.

-What are you saying?

-I may be infected.

-And, me? I've handled the case, too.

Octavio smiled with satisfaction.

-I assume that you are infected, as well.

Miss Kobe got up and paced her nicely furnished living room with the faux fireplace.

-That's not fair! I haven't killed anyone. You did it and that wasn't supposed to happen. You said that no one would be harmed. We'd simply barter the stone to the highest bidder. You said we'd take it on the international market.

-I lied.

-Bastard. And, now you've signed both our death warrants. Well, I may not be infected. I'll go to the nearest hospital right now and get tested. I don't want to die.

-You will stay right where you are. I've a brief but important call to make. Then, we will discuss my plans at length.

-What plans? You're a dead man, Louis. If the radiation doesn't get you, the police will.

-Will they?

-Yes. They're not as stupid as you think. They'll find you and burn you but good.

-And, what will your sentence be, my dear? Life in prison? You are an accomplice.

-No! Not anymore. I'll turn State's evidence.

-Don't even think of betraying me.

-You betrayed me! I don't owe you a damned thing. I'm putting on my coat and leaving. You can stay if you want. Finish the damned bottle and get plastered.

Eileen Kobe walked over to the clothes closet and picked out a coat and matching hat. She didn't hear Octavio coming up behind her because he'd taken off his shoes. With the blunt end of his gun, he struck her hard on the back of the head. She fell to the floor dazed but still alive.

Octavio took the silk scarf that she'd chosen to wear and wrapped it around her mouth to stifle any screams. He proceeded to kick the life out of her...first there were blows to the head to render his victim unconscious and then blows to every part of her inert body.

When he finished the job, he shoved the body into the closet and shut the door. He walked back into the living room and poured himself another drink.

Marlena and Susan arrived at Edward's office just as he and Yolanda were about to leave.

-Marlena, I'm on my way uptown. I can't stick around and talk.

-To see Lt. Donovan. I know what's happened, so I won't delay you. But, come to my townhouse tonight. We must talk. Much is at stake.

-I'll try and make it, but I can't make any promises. I'm going to drop Yolanda off first.

Marlena made a face. Yolanda wasn't one of Marlena's favorite people. And, Miss Lake had deliberately not invited the figure skater.

-Of course.

Edward buttoned up his coat and put on his Fedora.

-Ladies? Be careful.

-Edward, just one moment.

-Marlena, I've gotta' run.

-Susan and I were followed by a gray van this morning.

Edward stopped to listen.

-Did it try and catch up with you?

-No. It was a warning..

Edward was forced to agree.

-Listen, don't take any chances. Go straight home and stay there. I'll try to get to your place tonight. Now, I gotta' run.

Yolanda walked out with Edward glancing back at Marlena with a dirty look.

Marlena went over to Edward's desk and made herself at home.

-Mother? Turning private investigator?

-In a sense, my dear. I've always been an investigator of sorts. You do come close to the truth if somewhat haphazardly.

-Mother? I think we should drive Nella home. The trains aren't safe and the entire system might be shut down by now.

Nella protested.

-Susan, I'm sure I can get a cab. But, thanks, anyway.

Victoria was too much of a lady to say it; but, she didn't like Marlena.

It was just past noon when Edward reached the 86th St. precinct. He dropped Yolanda off and she made him a couple of "Johnny" cakes to take with him. He was just finishing off the second one as he locked his car door.

Three minutes later, he and Sgt. Rayno were sitting across from Lt. Donovan in the latter's small office. Alexandra Raymond was sitting on the window's ledge with a notepad and pencil instead of her usual stenotype machine.

Lt. Donovan began the proceedings.

-The Mayor has shut down the entire subway line and that includes all above ground transit buses, as well.

-That will paralyze the city.

-It will, Sgt. Rayno; but, it might also paralyze our killer's movements.

Edward spoke up.

-Or killers. Louis Octavio must be getting help from somewhere. This kind of terrorist act, and that's what I'm calling it, needs a lot of planning and organization. He couldn't carry it out by himself.

-But, where is he getting this help, Mendez? And, are we so sure that it is Louis Octavio? He's clean as far as we know. He's got no police record.

-I'd stake my P. I. license on it, Lieutenant. What did you turn up at his apartment?

-A subway map with just about every subway station marked off.

-Christ! And, you don't call that damning?

Miss Raymond spoke up.

-Were any stations *not* crossed off?

Lt. Donovan thought about this while banging his pack of cigarettes on his desk.

-No. I don't think so. But, the boys in forensics are going over it now. I'm with you, Mendez: Octavio's our man. What did you turn up at Montenegro's place?

-Ricardo Montenegro was abducted before we got there.

-You're joking? We didn't hear anything on that.

-You will, Lieutenant. And, I don't joke.

Sgt. Rayno asked a question.

-Did anyone see it happen?

Edward told them all about the neighbor who witnessed the abduction.

-Man! This case is getting real complicated.

Miss Raymond had to agree.

-Any idea who these men were in the gray van, Eddie?

-Miss Raymond, I wish I could answer that. But,I think I know someone who can.

Lt. Donovan took a cigarette out of the pack.

-Wouldn't be your friend, Marlena Lake?

-Bulls-eye, Lieutenant.

-What did you find in Montenegro's place?

-He had a visitor that morning or late last night.

-Octavio?

-Gotta' be. He kept a journal in his bedroom.

Miss Raymond shook her head.

-A dangerous thing to do.

Edward nodded.

-Agreed. He was going to turn "rat" on his buddies. I think he got cold feet about murder and that may be why he was taken. That entry was recent...maybe even just hours old. If Octavio saw it, he had to act on it

Lt. Donovan finished Edward's thought.

-Friend or no friend, Montenegro had to be eliminated. Kidnapping is clean and neat. He wouldn't have to concern himself with a corpse. But, let's get back to the subway bombing. Gentlemen and lady, any thoughts or insights?

Miss Raymond had a question.

-Lieutenant, was there any warning aside from the phone call to Ginny Gray?

-Not that we know of. And, I think we should keep Miss Gray near her phone in case of another call. We'll send some of the tech boys over and have it tapped.

Lt. Donovan continued while tapping ashes from his cigarette into the ashtray.

-I'm betting that there will be another call – there's bound to be a follow-up. So, we'll hold tight on that one. Alex? Get a hold of Ginny Gray and tell her to stay put. And, if she won't, contact her editor and tell him *not* to put her on any assignment – and that's a god-damned order.

-I've been trying to reach her all morning, but she *is* on assignment.

Edward laughed.

-Knowing Ginny, she's probably in the subway tunnel right now trying to push her way through every cop who stands between her and a scoop.

Lt. Donovan addressed Miss Raymond.

-Alex? Get on the phone and keep trying. Use the Interrogation Room.

Miss Raymond got off the window's ledge.

-I'm on it.

She excused herself with her usual smile.

Sgt. Rayno grinned.

-A real pretty girl.

Lt. Donovan and Edward didn't respond. The P. I. wanted to get a few things straight in his own mind.

-So far, we're working on the assumption that our culprit is Louis Octavio. So, let's put together a couple of more assumptions.

Lt. Donovan tapped some more ash into the ashtray.

-Like what? And, careful with your assumptions, Mendez. They could backfire real hard.

Edward exhaled some smoke in the Lieutenant's general direction.

-Let's assume that Louis Octavio planted the bomb – or whatever the hell it was -- which means that at one point he had to be a commuter on the LL train heading into Manhattan this morning. So where did he get on and at what station did he get off?. Because, unless this was a suicide mission, he had to get off no later than Lorimer St. which is the stop just before Bedford Ave. where the train enters the tunnel.

Lt. Donovan agreed. In spite of himself, he liked how the shamus' mind worked.

-Keep talking. We're with you so far.

Edward continued.

-Which means he wasn't riding alone. Even at the most ungodly hour, there's probably a couple of passengers in each and every car: night shift workers, homeless people. Which means that someone spotted – or even better – can identify Octavio. We just might be able to make up a composite image of the bastard and plaster it on the front page of every newspaper in the damned city.

-I like those assumptions, Mendez. Keep 'em coming.

-The trick is to figure out where Octavio got on and where he got off.

Lt. Donovan took out a subway timetable from his desk drawer.

-I know you'd *never* guess it, but the subway does run on a time schedule.

Sgt. Rayno laughed out loud.

-You're right, Lieutenant, I would've never guessed it.

Lt. Donovan opened the timetable and spread it across his desk. Edward and Sgt. Rayno got up and stood on either side of the Lieutenant.

-Lieutenant? You gotta' help me with this one. I'm real lousy at reading this kind of stuff.

Lt. Donovan pointed to the middle of the timetable.

-Here, Sergeant, that's the LL line. The explosion took place close to 8 A.M. in the connecting tunnel. The bomb must have been planted no later that 7:50 A.M. and that would be at the Bedford Avenue stop.

-That would make it a suicide mission.

-Right. So, it must have been planted at least a couple of stops prior to that one like Mendez here said. Maybe, at Graham Ave. which is not a transfer point.

Edward broke in.

-That's what I've been thinking. Octavio needed to get as far away from the detonation point as possible. Don't forget about the radiation fallout. From what I've been hearing, he'd have to put at least three stations between himself and the explosion.

Lt. Donovan continued.

-So, he'd have to get off no further down the line than Graham Ave. which is a non-transfer point. He'd either be stuck there or-

Edward finished the Lieutenant's sentence.

-Or he'd have to get out on to the street and cross over to the other side of the station to head in the opposite direction. That'd be taking a risk and gambling with valuable time.

-He might have had a car waiting for him.

Edward put out his cigarette.

-Maybe, Sergeant, or even a gray van. And, I'm betting on a gray van. I've been seeing too many of them, lately.

-A what?

-Montenegro was abducted and put into a gray van this morning.

Lt. Donovan put out his cigarette.

-Let's forget this gray van for now.

Edward shrugged his broad shoulders.

-Okay with me. My money is on a key transfer point. Don't forget, the train is getting more and more crowded at each stop. He's got to plant the bomb and, then, make his way out of the train which is not so easy during the rush hour – especially when you don't want to draw attention to yourself.

Sgt. Rayno grinned.

-Would it matter who noticed him getting out? All those people are gonna' be dead in a few minutes.

Edward took out another cigarette and continued.

-Let's assume – again! – that Octavio got on at Canarsie – the first stop on the line. He gets himself a seat.

Sgt. Rayno cut in.

-Why the first stop?

-To make sure that he gets a seat and positions himself in front of as few people as possible. And, to give himself time to make any last minute adjustments or changes. Remember, anything can go wrong. This gives him plenty of time to plant the device and choose his departure route.

-What transfer points do you have in mind, Mendez?

-Glad you asked, Lieutenant. My sister, Dottie, used to ride that line. The transfer stations I had in mind were Broadway Junction which happens to be above ground or Myrtle and Wyckoff Ave., both are transfer points and real busy during rush hour. And, the LL wouldn't be too crowded. He could get off without being conspicuous. He'd just be a commuter transferring to another line.

Lt. Donovan thought it over.

-Make sense...really good sense. So, how do we find this witness who can give us a description?

Edward went back to his chair.

-We're going to need the Mayor's help. He closed down the system; but, he's going to have to reopen it.

-That's not gonna' happen, Mendez.

-It's got to. I don't think Octavio's going to strike again until he makes some kind of demand. He knows that he can't push us too far.

-That's too big of an assumption. And, it's the LL line that's gotta' be reopened, so forget it for now. And, besides, the tunnel's structure's been compromised. It could crack open at any second.

-Why not open it up as far as the Myrtle and Wyckoff Ave. station?

Lt. Donovan shook his head.

-I'm not arguing with you, Mendez. But, I know this Mayor and so do you two gents. The transit system is staying closed, especially with the threat of radiation.

Edward was forced to agree; but, he had an alternate plan up his sleeve.

-How about we put out a radio bulletin every hour or half hour? Ask for witnesses to come forward. We can even put out squad cars along those key transfer points to canvas the area and put up bulletins. We can get this organized in just a couple of hours.

Lt. Donovan agreed. He was even enthusiastic about it.

-*That* we can do. Sgt. Rayno, start the ball rolling and get Miss Raymond to help and some of the on-duty officers. Get in touch with every precinct along the LL line and tell them what we're up to. Do it now, Sergeant.

Sgt. Rayno hurried out of the room.

-Lieutenant? When we get that call from Octavio – and I'm betting that we will – we'll know how much time we have.

-And, in the meantime, Mendez?

-I'm heading out to Canarsie and canvas the area myself. It'll give me something to do.

Eleven

EDWARD PARKED his car just across the street from the train station. He turned on the car radio. The P. I. listened to some Big Band music which was not his favorite, but it would do for the moment. He lit a cigarette. He was hoping that the token booth clerk was still on duty. But, what about the coming rush hour? How the hell were people supposed to get home? He put that thought out of his mind and got out of his Ford.

He walked over to the station holding on to his Fedora. The wind had picked up. He looked about the area: a couple of factories were nearby and the rest looked residential with a couple of apartment buildings thrown into the mix. A few teenagers were hanging around outside a candy store down the block.

Edward walked up the stairs to the elevated train platform and...yes! The clerk was still on duty.

-Good afternoon.

-Trains ain't running, Mister.

-I know. I'm not looking for a train. I'd like to talk to you.

-What about? You wouldn't be with the cops now, would you? Heard about that explosion in the tunnel. Terrible thing to happen. Couple of people 'round here think it's some kind of Commie plot.

Edward smiled. The thought of a Communist plot really wasn't so far fetched. It might even have a grain of truth to it. He heard the sound of a train approaching.

-It won't stop, Mister. Just passing through on its way to the yard.

Edward studied the man. He was about fifty-five with gray hair that was receding at the temples. He was wearing spectacles. He seemed like a good sort who was willing to be helpful if he could.

-Name's Edward Mendez. I'm a private investigator working with the police.

-Any news that I haven't heard on the radio?

-No. I think they've pretty well covered it.

-How can I help you, Mr. Mendez?

-You must see a lot of people coming through here every day. Mostly familiar faces, I bet.

-Mostly. But, a newcomer does come along once in a while.

-Mr.?

-Oh. Sorry about that. Barton Moran at your service.

-Barton, were there any newcomers this morning?

-Let me think for just a second. No.... Yes. There was one, Mr. Mendez. How could I forget? He was a tall figure of a fella'. Had on an overcoat and gloves. Real spiffy dresser.

-What else was he wearing?

-Scarf. It was a dark overcoat and one of those German style hats. In a big hurry, he was. He didn't actually come to my booth, mind you. I saw him walking on the train platform. Kinda' looked like he just got off the train coming in and was getting ready to board the one heading on out. He looked to be doing something.

-Doing what, Barton?

-Fiddling with a briefcase. Looked like an expensive one, too. I got an eye for the finer things.

Edward steadied himself.

-Barton, think...what did he look like? Any feature that someone would notice?

The clerk shook his head.

-You gotta' remember, Mr. Mendez, that this here was from a distance. He did turn around in my direction more than once. Let me see... Piercing eyes that kinda' looked through you. I don't think he wanted me to see his face

-And, he was carrying a briefcase.

-That I could swear to. It was on his lap. Can't blame him for that. Shouldn't put things on the floor. My wife never does and warns me not to. That's how they get stolen.

-I'll bet! Barton, you may have to come down to police HQ later. Don't be upset if you're approached by a police officer. And, try to remember anything else you can.

-Will do, Mr. Mendez. A pleasure.

-Same here.

Edward started back to his car when a voice stopped him.

-Mr. Mendez? It's Barton Moran, again.

-That was fast. What's up?

-A high school kid that I'm kinda' friendly with. He's sharp and curious...sometimes puts his nose in where it shouldn't be.

-What's his name?

-Don't know the surname.

-I'll take the first name.

-Arthur. I know he might have been on that train that pulled in this morning -- the one that your man was probably on. He was visiting his uncle in the city. Mind you, Arthur didn't get off here. He goes to school at some place down the line.

-Know where Arthur lives?

Barton Moran shook his head.

-Here 'bouts; but, I couldn't give you a street.

Edward looked down the street at the teenage boys.

-He wouldn't be one of those, would he?

-Can't really make out the faces; but, he just might be.

-Barton, you get back to your booth. And, thanks, again, pal.

Edward walked to the corner candy store. The teenagers were still there and flicking baseball cards. They stopped their game when the P. I. approached. Edward took out some chewing gum and stuck a piece in his mouth.

-Boys? Name's Edward Mendez. Would any of you happen to know a teenager by the name of Arthur?

One of the boys spoke up in a defiant voice. He was a kid with a crew cut and had elected himself as a spokesman for the group.

-What's he done?

-Not a thing, young man. I just happen to need his help.

-What kind of help you looking for, Mister?

Edward could see they were pretty harmless if a little arrogant and defensive.

-I'm working on a case that's pretty important. And, I could use Arthur's help if he's around.

The leader looked over toward the kid with the black, plastered hair and asked him.

-So, what do you think?

The kid with the slicked back hair spoke up.

-I'm Arthur, Mister. You a private dick or something?

Edward handed over his pack of gum to the "leader."

-Help yourselves. And, yes, Arthur, I'm a private investigator working with the police.

Edward now had Arthur and his friends' complete attention. And, Arthur was pretty eager to help.

-I'll bet I know what you want to know. It's about that man I talked to on the train this morning, isn't it?

-Tell me about that man, Arthur.

-He said he was a stock broker and heading out to see some customers. I thought people called up stock brokers and not the other way around.

-What else did he say?

-He wasn't trying to say anything. He didn't want to talk.

One of the teenage boys shouted.

-But, you twisted his arm!

Edward and Arthur ignored the boy's comment.

-Arthur, was he carrying anything with him?

-Yeah. He was. A briefcase. Nice. He was holding on to it pretty tight, too.

-Keep talking. You're doing just fine.

-Why you asking about him? Is it about that bomb going off in the subway tunnel? I'll bet it is.

The "leader" spoke up.

-Hey, Arthur, you better come clean, man.

Edward spoke.

-Where did he get off? Do you remember?

-Don't know. I got off before he did. He was still on the train. I'm pretty sure about that. But, wait...Mrs. Zimmerman could tell you. She got off at Myrtle and Wyckoff on the opposite side. She works in some ladies dress shop right on Myrtle Ave. She was just getting off her train as I was getting off of mine. I talk to her once in awhile. She's nice enough.

Edward had two more questions.

-Did the man mention his name?

-No. I didn't expect him to.

Another boy spoke up who was tall and had red hair.

-Is he the guy who blew up that train. Is he a Communist or something? Or maybe a Nazi? I hear there are some of them in hiding right here in America.

-Maybe to all three questions.

Arthur spoke up.

-He had initials on his briefcase in gold.

-Arthur, baby, what were they? Give!

-L.O.

Edward clenched his fist and patted Arthur roughly on the head.

-Man! Arthur, I want you to come with me.

-To the police?

-Yes. But, first we stop off at your place and let your mom know where we're going. Okay?

The P. I. spoke to the other boys.

-Gents? I want you to stick together and keep real quiet about this. Think you can do that?

Before anyone could answer, a shot rang out and Arthur fell to the pavement. The other teenagers fled for their lives down the block. Edward ducked behind a parked car and got off a couple of shots at a moving gray van. He was aiming for the rear tire, but just missed it.

The candy store owner ran out and knelt by Arthur whose plastered hair was smeared with blood and gray matter.

-My God! Who did this? Mister, did you see who did it?

-No. Is there a phone I could use in your store?

-Right inside.

-You tend to the boy. He might still be alive.

-Look at his head... My God! Arthur? Arthur, can you hear me?

Once inside the candy store, Edward dialed for an ambulance. Then, he placed a call to the 86th St precinct. Miss Raymond answered.

-Edward Mendez, Miss Raymond. Is Lt. Donovan or Sgt. Rayno there?

-Both are out on assignment.

-I don't have much time, so listen. Has anyone heard from Ginny Gray yet?

-Not yet. I was just trying to get a hold of her when you called, Eddie.

The familiarity didn't pass over Edward's head.

-I hope I'm not stepping on toes; but, it might be a good idea if you went to Ginny's office and sat at her desk until she gets there...whenever the hell that will be.

-I like that idea, Eddie. It's a good one. I'm on my way; but, some of the boys are already there.

-Miss Raymond, it'd be better if a female voice answered that phone. It might put Octavio off if he hears a man behind the receiver.

-You are smart. I'll get right down there as soon as I hang up with you.

-Hold up just one second, Miss Raymond.

-Alex. We're on the same team, aren't we?

-There's been an attempted homicide out here in Canarsie. A teenage boy by the name of Arthur-

Edward turned to the store owner who had come in.

-Hey, Mac, what's the kid's last name?

-Corelli. Arthur Corelli. He's dead.

A crowd was gathering outside the candy store and amongst them was a police officer.

Edward turned his attention back to his phone call.

-Arthur Corelli was his name. And, it's no longer an attempted homicide. The boy's dead. He had plenty to say before they gunned him down.

-Terrible. You're going to be tied up over there for a while then.

-Looks like it. I'll have to give my statement. And, by the way, Louis Octavio is our man, for sure.

Edward gave his statement to the Canarsie police. He didn't know the names of the other boys at the crime scene, but the candy store owner probably did. By this time, Lt. Donovan had gotten in touch with the Canarsie precinct and verified who Edward Mendez was. An A.P.B. was being put out.

Mrs. Harriet Zimmerman was escorted by patrol car to the precinct. She was upset about Arthur's death and wanted to do anything she could to help. She was the matronly sort, but well dressed and attractive. She'd gotten a lift home earlier that day because no one was sure when the trains would start up again. How people take the subway system for granted. Mrs. Zimmerman would never make that mistake again. Yes. She recalled the man who Arthur had spoken to and pointed out to her. Could she give a description of him? Of course.

She was in the clothing industry and sizing up people – if you'd pardon the expression – was her livelihood.

The man in question was tall and thin with a clear but sallow complexion. Thin lips and a Romanesque type nose...yes...it was big. Dark piercing eyes. You could tell that he took care of himself. In a good light, he could pass for a man in his forties; but, Mrs. Zimmerman was positive he was either pushing sixty or pulling on it. He was wearing a Hamburg hat, but she could see that he had salt and pepper hair. And, yes, the briefcase...it was a dark burgundy with gold trim. It looked rather thick. Dark overcoat and a matching suit. Wing tip shoes. Of course, she would guide the police sketch artist in his depiction. Oh, and by the way, this madman -- what else could he be? – looked rather nervous.

Edward spoke to the officer on duty.

-As soon as she's finished...

The two men suppressed a laugh. But at the same time, they were impressed with the woman who'd only gotten a cursory glance at Octavio.

-Send that sketch out to every paper in town and every precinct. But do me a favor?

-Name it.

-Send one copy straight off to the 86th St. precinct in Manhattan: attention Lt. William Donovan or I'll never hear the end of it.

-I understand. That'll be the first copy to go out.

-I owe you one, pal.

Twelve

EDWARD SWUNG his Ford on to Third Ave. and proceeded uptown. The time was closing in on 5 P.M. He just avoided an intense rush hour. Without the aid of the N.Y.C. Transit System, the traffic was fierce. Every cab in the city was taken and it looked like every car had hit the streets.

He pulled up in front of the 86th St precinct house and went straight on up to Lt. Donovan's office. Lt. Donovan was waiting for him along with Miss Raymond who had come back from Ginny Gray's office. Sgt. Rayno was in his patrol car on duty. The Lieutenant waved a copy of the police sketch of Louis Octavio.

-Have a look.

Edward took the sketch. Mrs. Zimmerman and the sketch artist had done a decent job. He took the chair next to Miss Raymond's and told his story.

-To my mind, the initials on the briefcase cinch it.

-Good work, Mendez.

Edward was curious.

-What happened at Ginny Gray's office, Miss Raymond?

-Alex. She finally came back. What held her up was decontamination. She and her photographer, Fred, I think his name is, had to go through a couple of hours of it. When I left he was developing photographs. No phone call came; at least, not when I was there.

Lt. Donovan put out his cigarette.

-So what the hell is Octavio waiting for?

-Maybe, he's got his own orders to follow.

-Whose orders?

-The men in the gray van. The ones who gunned down Arthur Corelli and followed Marlena Lake. The one I spotted outside my building. Let me see that sketch again, please.

Lt. Donovan handed it over.

-Here you go.

Edward examined the sketch.

-I've seen this character. Yesterday morning on the train heading downtown. He saw me, too. I spotted the bastard looking at me. Hold up! Today...I saw that bastard today down near Nassau St. I drove right past him.

-That's good, Mendez. That confirms this sketch's accuracy and the fact that he's still in the city. He's probably holed up someplace and biding his time.

-Should we notify police HQ downtown? We might just come up with Octavio himself.

-Get on it, Miss Raymond.

-I'm on my way.

-And, if you bump into Sgt. Rayno, send him on up.

-I will.

Miss Raymond left the office.

Lt. Donovan turned his attention to Edward.

-We're not doing half bad; but, I wish Octavio would make that call. He's got to, damn it.

-What about the radiation level in the subway tunnel? Any word on that?

-Not yet. But, tell me more about this gray van.

Edward shrugged his broad shoulders.

-Don't know anymore. I'm heading into Brooklyn and I might get a few answers.

-Good luck with that traffic outside.

Lt. Donovan had a thought as Edward was about to leave.

-Mendez, I take it you're going to question your mother some more about the stone. Take Miss Raymond with you. I want your mother's statements taken down verbatim. Normally, we'd have her in for questioning; but, I'm taking her age and health into consideration.

-I'm grateful, Lieutenant.

-Miss Raymond can take that machine of hers along and transcribe the notes here. Do you mind driving her back?

-Not at all. I'll be coming back to the city anyway.

-Good. And, if you have to, pressure your mother. We need answers.

Edward and Miss Raymond were facing Mrs. Mendez in her living room. She decided to leave her bedroom.

Miss Raymond finished setting up her stenotype machine and sat down next to Edward on the sofa. Mrs. Mendez sat in her usual armchair.

-Mrs. Mendez? I'm so sorry to hear about your daughter. It must be very difficult for you.

How many times must she hear these obligatory condolences? It was becoming tiresome.

-Thank you, Miss Raymond. An interesting machine you have there. Are you to take down my statements verbatim?

-Yes. But, just pretend that I'm not here. Sometimes my machine makes people a little nervous.

Mrs. Mendez was making Miss Raymond a little nervous. The matriarch had a penetrating gaze.

-Mother? This won't take long. Just a few questions.

-Is it a matter of life and death, Edward?

-Yes, it is.

-Then, we should begin.

-What do you know about the stone...or weapon, if you would...that Catrina stole from this house?

-The stones have been locked away in the cellar ever since.

Edward looked real hard at his mother.

-*Stones*? Just how many are there?

-Two stones of equal length.

-And, you-know-who has one, but who has the other stone?

-Most likely, a place called Romo-Ark.

Miss Raymond spoke up even though she shouldn't have.

-I've heard of them. They have headquarters right here in the city.

Mrs. Mendez nodded.

-They are an international corporation, my dear.

Edward resumed his questioning.

-And, mother, you think they may have the other stone? Because when I was down in the cellar that vault of yours was empty.

-Terrible. Terrible. What has Catrina done?

Edward felt his anger rising.

-Tell me, what exactly are these stones?

-They're an ancient artifact used in the War of the Gods. The ancient texts detail this war. The stones were stolen from the gods who were in reality extraterrestrials. They have been passed down through secret brotherhoods ever since. Your father was the last initiate to possess them.

-What did my father want you to do with them?

-To pass them on to his son.

-But, you didn't.

-You went into the Army and chose another path in life. You had to guide yourself to your intended destiny.

-Can the stones be destroyed?

Mrs. Mendez laughed.

-Only when they destroy half the world. They must be either buried in the deepest crevice in the earth or somehow propelled into the sun.

-Mother, the authorities should have been notified about this long ago. You know that.

-To what end, Edward? To examine them? Unthinkable. Any tampering with them would trigger off the radiation.

Mrs. Mendez took a deep breath and continued.

-Edward, would anyone have believed me? An occultist's gift from a secret brotherhood? Wars of the Gods of heaven? We would be laughed at.

-You've got a point there. Just one more thing...some gray vans have been spotted in the city lately. I saw one myself parked right outside my office building. Would you know anything about this?

-They target people. And, when those people have been targeted, they either disappear or are found dead.

-Who operates them? What's their home base?

-Trained killers operate them. Men who are outcasts from society. Their home base? I really don't know. I don't want to know. I have reason to believe that Romo-Ark is involved.

Edward took a deep breath.

-I think that just about does it for now.

He turned to Miss Raymond.

-You got all that?

-Every incredible word. You're very articulate, Mrs. Mendez. You've made my job easy.

-You're very gracious, young lady.

Mrs. Mendez left the room.

Miss Raymond handed over her typed transcript to Lt. Donovan. He read through it twice.

-Reads like some Hollywood movie: complete with an eccentric matriarch and a doomsday weapon.

He tossed the transcript on to his desk.

-Who the hell is gonna' believe this? I'm even having a hard time with it.

Miss Raymond picked up the transcript.

-It's pretty incredible all right. Mrs. Mendez believes what she's saying. I can tell you that much.

-And, what about Mendez?

-I'm not so sure. I got the impression that he thought his mother was holding back. Was his dad, Manuel Mendez, an actual occultist?

-And, the head honcho of some secret brotherhood from what I've gathered.

-That's incredible. Eddie seems so down to earth.

-His methods are pretty solid. And, he's a damned good private dick.

-But?

-You know the story. Stay with him.

Thirteen

A LONG day for Edward Mendez was almost at an end. He was sitting in Marlena's living room sipping a much needed whiskey and soda and admiring the new decor.

-Is Susan behind the redecorating? Nice job...cozy and warm and...

-Sedate?

-That's it.

-You look tired, Edward.

-Not too tired. But, I could sure use this. Where's Susan?

-Fixing dinner.

-I'm starved. Could use a good meal, too.

He swirled the whiskey in his glass. He felt like taking off his shoes, but resisted the temptation.

-Marlena?

-Yes, dear boy?

-Tell me all you know about these gray vans.

Marlena belted down her bourbon.

-First, tell me about your day and in detail. What do you know of the Diamond District murders and that dreadful subway tunnel explosion.

-I thought we'd gone through that.

-Only in a general sense. You know how detail oriented I am.

The P. I. filled his hostess in on everything. Whatever else she was, Marlena Lake could keep a secret...and she had lots of them.

Susan came into the room wearing an apron.

-Susan, take off that apron and join us for drinks.

-Why thank you, mother.

-And, freshen our drinks while you're at it like a good girl.

-Of course. Edward, what are you having?

-Whiskey and soda..

Edward turned back to his hostess.

-Marlena? These gray vans?

-When one is followed by one, it's either a warning or certain death. That man, Montenegro, you can assume that you'll never see him again. He's either dead or better off dead. They kill with intent and are very good at what they do.

Edward was starting to relax.

-So, who exactly are "they?"

Susan brought over the drinks and, then, sat down next to Edward.

-Do you know, mother?

-Agents. Saboteurs of some government agency...an agency that extends throughout the world.

-A government that's underground, you mean. A government that's not really a government at all? Maybe some international conglomerate? Do I have to mention a name?

-You understand the sub-context of my answer, dear boy.

Susan spoke up.

-How long have these agents been around?

-Their mode of transportation has changed to suit the context of the time period. They've been with us always. Their main purpose, I believe, is to temper mankind's advancement or to stifle it and bring about another Dark Age.

Edward wasn't impressed.

-Who controls whom?

Marlena looked at her favorite guest.

-At the moment, I don't know. But, these stones...their destructive power has been exploited, but what of its constructive power?

Edward finished his second whiskey and soda.

-I don't follow you, Marlena.

-Couldn't these stones be used as an energy source? Say a propellant or as a source of infinite light and heat?

-Maybe. But would we know how to use it without blowing ourselves to kingdom come? Do we have the technology to "tame" it?

Marlena sat forward in her chair.

-Excellent point, Edward. And, in answer to your question: no.

Ginny Gray was sitting at her desk and typing away like a bat-out-of-hell when the phone call came through at a quarter past ten.

-Ginny Gray here.

-We spoke this morning, Miss Gray.

Ginny waved frantically to the three police officers who had replaced Miss Raymond. Their tracking equipment was in place. A police officer stood over Ginny and motioned for her to keep him talking.

-I'll say we have. You've had quite a day for yourself – killing a couple of hundred people – that takes time and gall!

The police officer whispered in Ginny's ear.

-Don't antagonize him.

-Listen carefully, Miss Gray, or there will be another explosion and many more lives will be taken.

-I'm listening. That's my job.

-The sum of ten million dollars in untraceable notes is to be delivered by Edward Mendez tomorrow at dusk in Central Park.

-That's a mighty big place. Where, exactly?

-By the outcropping of bedrock just parallel to West 67th St.

-You said dusk. What time exactly? I need a time.

-You do not.

Ginny put on her most nonchalant but challenging voice.

-Why ten million? Why not be original about this? How about our dear Mayor's head on a silver platter? What say?

-You have your instructions and they are simple enough.

-And, just what do we get out of all this? You get the money and we get...

-The detonation stone. And, you are welcome to it.

-You hand over the doomsday stone when we hand over the money? And, you're in plain sight all the time?

-Is that not what I said?

-No. It's not what you said which is why I'm asking. Don't get cozy with me.

-Miss Gray, if there is any betrayal, I will carry out my threat. I've nothing to lose and we both have something to gain.

Ginny was about to speak when she heard the click on the other end of the line. She slammed down the phone and turned to face the police officer.

-Did you trace it?

The officer who'd been standing next to her rushed over to his two colleagues. In a couple of minutes, he turned back to Ginny.

-Got him!

Three police cars converged in front of the Gold St. apartment house of Eileen Kobe. Four officers in riot gear stormed up the front staircase followed by a medical team equipped with a Geiger counter.

A young, blonde woman opened her apartment door on the third floor and peered out.

-What the hell's going on here? Is this some kind of raid?

-Are you Eileen Kobe?

-No. It's that door just down the hall. What's she done?

-Get back inside your apartment and lock your door, Miss. Now!

Veronica Crane did as she was ordered. Why should she care about Eileen Kobe? Never liked the bitch.

The first officer pounded on the apartment door.

-Police! Open up!

No response.

-Open up! Now!

No response.

He looked back at his two fellow officers.

-Get ready.

They drew their guns.

The first officer was a black belt in karate. With one round-house kick, he broke open the door. He squatted down and moved quickly into the apartment. His fellow officers followed him in. The lights were turned off but light from the street lamps was filtering in through the Venetian blinds.

The first officer gave the order.

-Check that room out. I'll take the one straight ahead.

Kitchen, bathroom, bedroom and living room were checked out. Nothing. The second officer pointed to a clothes closet.

-Hey, chief, how about this closet over here?

The three officers moved toward it staying out of a direct line of fire in case someone was hiding behind the door. The first officer reached for the door knob, turned it and flung it open.

-Christ!

The body of Eileen Kobe was on the floor.

-Beaten to death. Call the meat wagon for this one. Holy crap! Looks like every bone in her body's been busted.

The contamination squad was in the living room. The three police officers heard a clicking sound that sounded like radio static.

-What the hell is that?

The three officers turned away from the corpse. The first officer asked.

-What's up?

The head man of the contamination unit responded.

-There are signs of radioactivity here. Not lethal, mind you, but you might want to evacuate the residents just in case. We need to check out the rest of the apartment, but so far the readings are stable and not in the red zone.

-The ambulance boys are downstairs.

-Good. Tell them to remove that body to a quarantine area.

The second officer ran down the stairs to the waiting ambulance. The third cop stayed with the contamination unit.

The first officer went knocking on residents' doors. Veronica Crane opened up.

-So, what gives? Eileen Kobe in some kind of trouble?

-She's dead. Murdered.

Miss Crane clutched at her robe.

-Oh gosh! How? When?

-Never mind that. Just pack a few things and visit a family member or a friend for a few days.

-You mean right this minute?

-Yes. I do, Miss.

-What's going on? I guess I can visit my Mom for a couple of days in Staten Island. Can I take my cat with me?

-Sure. If you need any help, we can drive you to your mom's place.

-That's real decent of you, officer. I didn't know that Eileen chick too good. The stand-offish type, if you know what I mean. And always nervous and looking over her shoulder. You'd think someone was out to get her- and, I guess they were. Poor kid.

-Did she have many friends?

-Only that one guy with his briefcase. Always carrying that briefcase like there was gold in it or something.

This first officer was up on his current events.

-Can you identify this boyfriend?

-He didn't act like a boyfriend...more like some co-conspirator. I picked that up from the movies. He gave me the creeps. But, I can point him out for you. He was with her tonight, as a matter of fact. I saw him come in- hey, you're not telling me that he was the one who bumped her off? He didn't look so hot himself. All sweaty and he had that briefcase with him. So what else is new?

-Miss...

-Veronica Crane. I work at the telephone exchange up on 14th and Lex.

-Get your things together and your cat.

The police officer looked past Miss Crane.

-Is that him?

-Isn't he adorable? He's only got the one eye, but he's real good company. An elderly lady passed away a few weeks ago in the building and I took him in.

-I'm gonna' alert the other tenants. I'll come back for you.

-Wait just a sec'. Do you think Mr. Briefcase did her in? You can level with me. He sure looked the type with those coal, black eyes of his. Gave me the willies.

-When did he get here tonight?

-After five. I couldn't pinpoint a time for you.

-Did you see him leave the building?

-I did at that. Me and Tommy were by the window just looking out when he came out. He started down the block in a hurry, like. But, it was kind of odd. This gray van caught up to him and he went around to the back of it and got in.

The phone rang and Susan answered it.

-Edward? It's for you.

He took the phone.

-Edward Mendez.

-Listen up.

Lt. Donovan gave the P. I. a complete update including the murder of Eileen Kobe and the Louis Octavio call to Ginny Gray.

Edward hung up the phone and walked back into Marlena's living room.

-Edward, dear boy, one for the road?

-No, thanks, Marlena. I'm heading downtown and traffic might still be heavy.

-And, the latest developments?

He sat down and gave his hostess an update.

-Another woman beaten to death down on Gold St. Louis Octavio seen leaving the building and an eyewitness to confirm it.

-Louis Octavio is the murderer of your sister and this Kobe woman. And, now he's demanding a king's ransom.

-That just about sizes it up. But, there's one interesting factor- You know, Marlena, on second thought, I think I will have one for the road.

-Of course.

Susan went to the drinks table to pour the P. I. another whiskey and soda.

-This Octavio got into a gray van.

-Indeed. Willingly or forced?

-It was waiting for him. He got in and it drove off to only-God-knows-where.

-Louis Octavio is not acting alone. He couldn't be.

Susan handed Edward his drink.

-Here you go. There's just a touch of whiskey in it. After all, you do have to drive.

-Thanks, Susan.

-So, dear boy, what's our next move?

Edward smiled and made a mock toast.

-That's easy. I've got a date with Octavio tomorrow at dusk in Central Park. Wish me luck.

-Of course, dear boy. And, don't be too surprised if a gray van shows up.

December 3, 1948
Fifth Ave. Skyscraper

Fourteen

IT WAS still dark when Louis Octavio awakened from his drugged sleep. He was slumped over the desk in the office of...whom? He only half remembered being taken to a skyscraper sometime late last night...it had to be last night. Surely, an entire day and night couldn't have gone by. He had to make certain.

Octavio pushed himself into an upright position and suffered a momentary sensation of vertigo. It passed. He placed his hands to his face and there was very little stubble. Good. Only a few hours had passed.

He looked about the unfamiliar office. The desk where he was sitting was executive style and in good condition. There were two leather chairs facing the desk, the obligatory potted plant in the corner, and a few framed nondescript pictures on the wall.

The room was dark. He reached for the desk lamp and pulled the dangling chain. It didn't go on. He got up and walked over to the door where there should be a light switch on the wall. He flipped it on. No light.

He tried the door. It opened to a receptionist's area. He went back to the desk. Where was his briefcase? He glanced out the window.

-How high up am I?

He leaned on the window sill. It was a straight drop down of about fifty stories. He turned away from the window and started searching for his briefcase. By this time, his eyes had grown accustomed to the darkness and the night sky was starting to give way to the daylight.

-Where is it?

He looked up. Had he heard a movement in the room? He looked out the window, again.

-That's the main branch of the public library over there. This must be-

-The 50th floor of 500 5th Ave., Mr. Octavio.

Octavio spun around to face that cold voice.

-Who are you?

-Here's your briefcase, you traitor. You really shouldn't be carrying it about with you. It could so easily be misplaced or stolen.

-I can't see you properly. Show yourself.

The man came forward.

-I still can't make you out.

-Take this briefcase, you fool.

He took the briefcase from the outstretched hand and placed it on the desk.

-Open it and check the contents.

He did as ordered. The man facing him was wearing a black suit and hat and his face was pale as chalk Was

he wearing sunglasses, as well?. He checked the contents of the briefcase . Nothing had been tampered with.

-Satisfied, Mr. Octavio?

-Yes. Thank you.

-Good. You will meet with Edward Mendez as planned. In the meantime, here are some further instructions. And, this time, do as you are ordered. Suspicion must be kept away from the company.

Naked, Edward got out of bed and went to the bathroom to relieve himself. When he walked back into the bedroom with a semi-erection, Yolanda was awake. He slipped into his boxer shorts. There was no time for love making this morning.

-I'll put the coffee on while you wash up.

-Thank you, my darling.

While the coffee was brewing, Edward got the bacon and eggs ready. He was hungry and he knew that Yolanda had a healthy appetite, as well. She was an athlete in training and needed to eat. He set the table and finished dressing. He had to meet with Lt. Donovan and the Chief of Police to go over the strategy for that rendezvous at dusk. It was only 5 A.M....about eleven hours away from his meeting with Octavio.

Yolanda came to the table buttoning her blouse.

-Smells delicious. I'll serve.

-Did you get last night's edition of the paper?

-It's on the couch. It was all about the subway tunnel bombing. The Diamond District murders were pushed back to page nine. But, Edward, why does it have to be you to meet with that madman?

-Right now, baby, he's calling the shots...that is, up until meeting time. We've got a few surprises for him.

-It sounds too risky to me. Here's your eggs.

-Thanks, baby.

-Can he be trusted to keep his end of the bargain?

-I'm betting that he can't.

-Will he have the stone – or whatever it is – with him?

-We're not counting on it.

-Maybe, he'll make more demands. Blackmailers always do, you know.

-He might.

-Edward, what aren't you telling me?

-What I've been ordered not to. Believe me, it's for your own good.

-I trust you; but, I don't trust this Octavio.

-You've got plenty of company there, baby.

-Where will you be all day?

-At the 86th St. precinct house with our friend, Lt. Donovan. Sgt. Rayno oughta' be there, too, along with the Chief of Police. What time do you plan on getting back here?

-Around three o'clock.

-Might be a good idea to stay indoors today as much as possible.

-I'll be worrying about you all day.

-I'll be kind of worried myself. But, don't worry too much. We're gonna' be prepared for the bum.

Edward arrived at the 86th St. precinct at 7 A.M. sharp which was approximately nine hours before his meeting with Louis Octavio. How the hell was he going to get through that time? He didn't know it when he walked into Lt. Donovan's office, but the time was gonna' tick by real fast.

-Mendez, sit down. We'll have company pretty soon and, then, we'll move into the Interrogation Room upstairs.

Edward took off his coat and Fedora.

-Getting pretty cold out there.

-I'll say! It was below freezing when I got up and it's still not officially winter.

-You just reminded me, Lieutenant, about something I've got to ask Marlena about. Funny how I forgot about it last night.

-Miss Lake? You keep in touch with her a lot, don't you?

-She keeps in touch with me. But, what I'm thinking about now has nothing to do with today.

-She knows about the dusk rendezvous with Octavio, I take it.

It was a statement.

-She does. And, she warned me not to trust him.

-I'd have to agree with her on that.

-She's also worried about Octavio's cohorts.

-We don't know for sure that he has any.

-He had at least two: Eileen Kobe and Ricardo Montenegro.

-And, they're both dead...at least, Kobe is. I wish we could get a lead on this mysterious gray van.

-Marlena thought that it might show up today.

-Oh, did she? That woman knows too much for her own good.

Sgt. Rayno walked in.

-Lieutenant? Oh, hi, Eddie. The Chief of Police is upstairs. Oh, and Ginny Gray is pacing around upstairs, too.

-Tell them we're on our way, Sergeant.

In the third floor Interrogation Room, Edward was being briefed by the Chief of Police.

-Mr. Mendez, your radiation gear is all set and ready for you to put on. We'll take you as far as West 67th St. and Central Park West. You'll have a Geiger counter just in case.

-Won't that kind of weigh me down?

-It will until the Geiger counter takes its reading and if it's safe, you can discard. Don't try to take the stone out of the briefcase.

-That's after I've checked to see if the stone is there. That diamond cutter, Eisenstein, probably cut it into at least two pieces. But, I pretty much know the general size of the thing.

-Good. Check it out, but don't *take* it out.

Edward took out his pack of Lucky Strike.

-Your men will be there, Chief?

The Chief of Police sat back with a Cheshire smile on his ruddy but handsome face.

-Oh, yes. The minute Miss Gray hung up with that killer, approximately one hundred men were dispatched: undercover surveillance, you might say. You won't see them, Mr. Mendez, but they'll be there and they're the best we've got..

-But, will Octavio spot them?

-That scum won't know what hit him. He'll see you in full operational gear so he should be focused on *you*.. You'll test for any radiation and, if it's too "hot," you get the hell out of there – pronto! No heroics, Mr. Mendez.

-And, if it tests okay?

-Drop the Geiger counter and unsuit. You'll be the closest one to Octavio, so you'll stand the best chance of taking him down. It's a safe bet that he won't be handing over all the stuff. He can't. Why would he want to? Makes no sense. Holding out on us is his only way out.

Ginny Gray broke into the conversation.

-And, if he's holding out, Chief? Then, what? You bring him down here?

-Miss Gray, we'll do a lot more than just talk to him. We've got our methods and don't ask for the details.

Lt. Donovan shook his head.

-Just supposing that Octavio doesn't show? Supposing that someone else does?

Ginny Gray once again joined in.

-That's just what I was thinking. Suppose it's all a set up?

Sgt. Rayno spoke up.

-Who else would show up?

The Chief of Police answered Sgt. Rayno.

-Don't know, Sergeant. But, why would Octavio stick his neck out like this? If he's handing over all the stuff, he'd have to bluff his way out. And, maybe, that's what he's counting on: our not taking any chances that there's more of that stuff out there ready to go off.

The Chief of Police turned his attention back to Edward.

-Anyway, Mr. Mendez, they'll be undercover cops all over the place. The park has been closed off to the public and every available patrol car will have the damned place surrounded tighter than a conga drum.

Mrs. Mendez joined her three daughters for lunch.

Dottie buttered her toast.

-Mother, what are you thinking about?

-Your sister, of course. And, your brother, Edward. Ladies? Has Edward asked you about her at all?

Victoria put down her coffee cup.

-He asked about her friends, mother. I only know of two: Linda and Rachel. Were there any others?

The old lady nodded.

-No. I don't think so. Catrina introduced me to Linda and Rachel when she first brought them over. I didn't think very much of them at the time.

Dottie almost choked on her slice of buttered toast.

-What? An indirect criticism of your darling daughter, Miss Catrina. Heavens! Why didn't you like them? Come on, mother, out with it.

-I thought them rather silly and insincere.

-Never met them. Not that I'm sorry for it.

-Dottie, I met them – well, saw them. Catrina never actually introduced us.

-Well that figures, Victoria. She wouldn't.

-Why was your brother asking about them, Victoria?

-He just wanted to know if Catrina had any friends.

Mrs. Mendez stirred the milk in her coffee.

-Someone whom she might have confided in. Yes. I can understand your brother wanting to know that.

Nella posed her question.

-Just out of curiosity, what were their last names? Victoria, do you know?

-I've no idea. Mother? How about you?

-Let me think. It's such a long time ago.

Nella pressed her mother for an answer.

-It might be important. I think Eddie would like to know.

-Must you call Edward by that ridiculous nickname?

The three sisters waited.

-Yes. I have it. Linda Silverman and Rachel Schwartz. I wonder what ever became of them.

Dottie wiped the butter from her mouth.

-Don't worry, mother, Eddie will find out.

Fifteen

IT WAS 3:30 P.M. and Edward was being police escorted to the west side of Central Park. There was a layer of gray clouds hovering over the city, but no threat of snow until later that evening.

The driver, Lt. Donovan, Sgt. Rayno and Edward said little on the trip to the drop off point. The mechanics and sequence of events were gone over thoroughly several times at the precinct. The drive itself was the most trying and nerve wracking time. They took the cut-off point into the park at 72nd St.

-Okay, Mendez, as soon as we get out of this car, you suit up. You'll be a little early but that should be okay with Octavio. And, if it's not...tough!

Edward grinned.

-Sort of puts his mind at ease. But, Lieutenant, how is Octavio going to arrive? Will the cops just let him walk in? Why not just grab him?

-We thought of that; but, he might just panic and blow up half the city.

-That answers my second question. What about the first one?

-Don't know. Maybe that gray van will drop him off or place him right on the rendezvous point. Just get that briefcase from him. And, remember, we can't let him get away.

Edward stood on the exposed bedrock. There was a stillness in the dusk that was unnerving...like the unnatural stillness before an earthquake or some terrible upheaval. He stood there suited up and with a Geiger counter in his right hand. His gun was in its shoulder holster and he had one extra gun tucked into the back of his trousers. He was ready. So where was Octavio?

Wast it a set up as Ginny Gray had thought? And, was he, Edward Mendez, the patsy? He felt overheated in his radiation gear. The park was so damned quiet. He saw pigeons flying overhead but couldn't hear their cooing or fluttering. Even the "stop motion" movement of the squirrels wasn't making a sound.

Then, Edward saw the gray van coming toward him. Even that was noiseless. Had he gone deaf? The van drew closer and ...yes! He heard the tires moving over the gravel. It came within twenty feet of where he stood and jerked to a stop. The two back doors opened up and a man holding a briefcase stepped out. The man came within three feet of Edward and stopped. It was Louis Octavio.

-Mr, Mendez, do you have the money?

-It's right here.

The P. I. put down the heavy duffel bag and pushed it toward Octavio.

-Take it. Take your blood money.

Edward turned on the Geiger counter and there was only a slight reading...a crackling.

-And, here is the weapon.

Octavio handed Edward the briefcase. Edward noted Octavio's initials in gold.

-Take it, Mr. Mendez, and check the contents.

-I will.

Edward opened the flap of the leather briefcase and took out the lead box. The Geiger counter was still on and its "crackling" increased, but it still registered in the "green." And, now came the most dangerous of this most deadly game: opening the lead lined box. The P. I. flipped it open. Inside were two pieces and half of a third. The Geiger counter went haywire. He slammed the box shut and the Geiger counter reading went back into the safety zone. He stood up and took off his head-gear.

-Is there a piece missing? What gives, Octavio? You trying to pull a fast one?

-A fragment of that piece has already been detonated, as you know.

-So, where's the rest? Are there any more "fragments?" You holding out for more money?

-They are.

-Who are "they?"

Edward took off the rest of his radiation gear. His hands were now free and he could move about a lot faster.

-They are killers, Mr. Mendez. Anarchists who trade in blood. They are an international network of cut throats who will be with us until doomsday.

-So, why hand over most of the goods?

-Their takeover time was not yet arrived.

Edward moved a step closer.

-Not on my watch, pal. Who gives these goons their orders?

-I don't know.

-I think you do know, Octavio.

Silence.

-So, where's the rest of it? That's the second time I've had to ask you that question...so, answer it!

-Mr. Mendez, stay vigilant. They have encountered difficulty in this great country of America. You are a resilient and fierce people...stay that way.

-We don't plan to change. Now, why give back this dynamite?

-They know that your government won't use it.

Edward picked up the briefcase.

-I can't just let you walk off.

-I'm a dead man, no matter what.

-If you're looking for an argument, change the subject. And, we're wasting time. Once again...are there any more of these fragments?

-In place.

-What? Explain that, pal.

Octavio looked over his shoulder at the gray van. A squirrel raced by followed by another squirrel. He backed away from Edward and, then, broke into a run.

A dozen undercover cops came into view, emerging from their camouflaged hiding places...against trees, on tree branches and seemingly coming out from under the ground itself. Edward handed over the briefcase to the nearest cop and took off after Octavio who hadn't gotten very far. An undercover cop had him on his knees and was cuffing him.

The gray van started forward, but it was sprayed with a few dozen bullets. The van's wheels were blown out and its front windshield shattered...killing the driver and the man sitting in the passenger seat.

Edward and two other officers ran to the back of the van and pulled open the double doors. A man in a black suit lay dead on the floor. The man was shot in the head. He had taken his own life. The P. I. turned away from the dead man and walked over to the now handcuffed Octavio who looked eager to talk.

-I must speak with you, Mr. Mendez.

-Then, why did you run away just now?

-Fear, Mr. Mendez. A trapped man has fear that can take on any irrational behavior.

-We'll do our talking at the precinct house. Get up.

-That will do. And, perhaps, a deal?

-Forget it. No deals.

The handcuffed man looked at the gray sky overhead.

-Even a dying man such as myself wants to live for as long as he can.

Lt. Donovan came running up to the three men.

-Nice work, Mendez. You too, officer.

The Lieutenant turned to face Octavio.

-Okay, pal, I've got a few questions for you. You're not looking any too good. Let's go. We'll give you a couple of aspirin.

-The pieces have been hauled off to Aberdeen. Any more than that, I can't tell you. Now, what's this about missing pieces?

That was the Chief of Police speaking. He was about to question Octavio, but Edward spoke up.

-Mr. Octavio here told me that other pieces were planted..."fragments". Isn't that right? That is what you said?

-Yes.

The Chief of Police took over, again.

-Where? Somewhere in the city? You can tell us.

-Yes.

-Where in the city? Talk.

-I want to make a deal.

-Forget it. We don't make deals with mass murderers.

Miss Raymond came in and addressed the Chief.

-You're wanted on the phone, sir.

-Thank you. Excuse me, please.

He left the Interrogation Room.

Lt. Donovan spoke to Miss Raymond, but his gaze never left Octavio.

-Miss Raymond? Get your stenotype machine and come right back.

-You bet.

Lt. Donovan addressed the group.

-We'll wait for Miss Raymond to return. I want a transcript of this meeting. I want to immortalize you...you fucking murderer.

They didn't have to wait long. Miss Raymond came back in with her stenotype machine.

-I'm ready, Lieutenant.

-Good. So you want to cut a deal, Mr. Octavio?

-Yes.

-What kind of deal? And, my listening to it doesn't mean I agree to it.

-I will tell you where the remaining pieces have been planted. Just let me go with the sum of one million dollars.

-I wouldn't give you money for a subway token.

-You have no choice. And, I will tell you this: I didn't plant them. It was those assassins in black suits who did the job.

-Buddies of yours, huh? And, they told you where they hid the bomb? I don't believe you. Why would they tell you when chances are you'd be caught?

-I...

-Go ahead, talk. Talk!

-I can surmise where at least one is. There may be more. I'll be honest. I don't know.

Lt. Donovan laughed and so did Edward. Sgt. Rayno and Ginny Gray kept a poker face.

-You don't know?

-I know where at least one may be hidden.

-Where?

-Deal?

-No.

Edward spoke up.

-Can you "guess" where this other one might be planted?

Ginny Gray spoke for the first time.

-He's bluffing. I don't think he knows anything. Do you, Octavio? You're a tool that's been used and tossed into the trash heap. You're finished. Kaput!

Octavio chose his words carefully.

-I don't know; but, someone who I've never met might have that knowledge.

Edward waved an admonishing finger at Octavio

-Like Ginny just said, he's bluffing. If you knew, pal, you'd cough it up.

Ginny lit a cigarette and noticed that the Lieutenant was staring directly at her.

Edward kept prodding Octavio.

-Who? Come on, Octavio, I'm running out of cigarettes. I'm gonna' have to bum one off of Miss Gray here.

Lt. Donovan broke in.

-Where's the first one and when is it set to go off? You tell us that and you might –might – get a deal.

Octavio realized that Lt. Donovan was a hard man to bargain with.

-You win. They had me in an office in midtown from last night until the rendezvous time.

Lt. Donovan pointed his cigarette at him.

-Where, damn it! Before I use your hand as an ashtray. Talk and stop stalling!

Ginny patted the Lieutenant on the shoulder.

-Easy, Lieutenant. He's starting to melt.

-At the 500 5th Ave. skyscraper on the 50th floor. That's where they held me. I swear that's the truth.

-When is it set to go off?

-Sometime before midnight. I can't be sure. I was once a confidante of theirs but no longer. Send your men there at once in radiation suits. There's no time to lose...and be careful bringing it down.

Lt. Donovan ordered Sgt. Rayno to give the order...pronto! The Sergeant practically ran out of the room.

-Okay, Octavio, where's that other piece? And, if you don't know, who does?

-What about our deal?

Lt. Donovan stood up and tossed his cigarette in Octavio's face.

-We've got no deal! But, let me put it on the line to you. You've killed at least five hundred people, not counting Eileen Kobe and Catrina Mendez. Now, you've got a chance to save some lives. You gonna' take it? You've taken a first step, now take that second one, pal.

-It will be a suicide mission. The carrier may not even know she has it.

The Lieutenant was now standing over Octavio.

-"She?" Who is it?

-I- I ruined their plans...my greed ruined their plans. I was punished for that.

Octavio collapsed to the floor. Miss Raymond got up and went to the door.

-I'll get the medics.

Ginny Gray shouted over.

-And, a Geiger counter. Who knows how "hot" this guy is.

Miss Raymond nodded and left the room.

Edward went over to the fallen man and knelt down.

-He's out like a light.

Lt. Donovan didn't move from his chair.

-I'd say he's about ready for the morgue.

Edward took out a cigarette, lit up and got to his feet.

-We'd better keep clear of him.

Ginny tried laughing, but couldn't quite manage it.

-I've got a better idea, boys. Let's get the hell out of here! This bum's beyond our help.

Lt. Donovan agreed with the ace reporter.

-Like I said, he's about ready for the file cabinet.

Edward got the door opened.

-The guy's heart was practically pounding out of his chest.

The two men and Ginny Gray left the Interrogation Room with Louis Octavio close to death.

Sixteen

THE FOUR squad cars converged on 500 5th Ave. Sixteen cops got out and went phalanx style into the main lobby of the building. The information clerk and the guard on duty were told by Sgt. Rayno in a tone of voice that was not to be questioned:

-Clear the lobby. Now!

The guard started clearing the people from the lobby – those by the concession stand and those waiting for elevators to arrive.

The police outside formed a human gauntlet to get people out of the immediate area and off the block altogether. Despite this, curious onlookers gathered across the street.

Inside the building, Sgt. Rayno and his men were waiting for their elevator that would take them directly up to the 50th floor.

-Come on, already.

Another officer was with him and two men in radiation gear.

-Is the damned thing stuck?

-It's coming down, Sergeant. What happens when we get up there?

-We take every inch of that floor apart. And, I mean *everything* – carpets, desk drawers, paintings...everything. And, just pray we're in time.

-Or?

-Or we'll be blown sky high with the top half of this building.

-Sorry I asked.

The elevator arrived and the four men got in.

-Press for the 50th floor, officer.

The elevator started up.

-Sgt, Rayno?

-What is it?

-What happens when we find it? This thing is "hot."

-If you spot it, mover away real quick and alert these two boys right here.

The elevator passed the 20th floor.

-We're almost halfway there.

Sgt. Rayno turned to the two technicians.

-You boys all set? Once we find this- this bomb, we've gotta clear it out, pronto. The demolition truck should be arriving any second now. Once we hit the 50th floor, we'll put this elevator on hold.

-What about the tenants in the building? Shouldn't they be evacuated?

-No time and it would only cause panic and get in the way of our own operation. Every damn second counts here.

-Look. We just passed the 40th floor. My ears just popped.

-Start getting ready, boys. You know which office we go into first.

-To the right as we step off.

The office door was locked. Sgt. Rayno took out his gun and blasted the lock open and kicked in the door.

-Okay. Go to it!

Sgt. Rayno went straight to the room where Octavio had been. He pulled open every desk drawer and ransacked through it. Then, he pulled it out, flipped it over and tossed it to the floor. He checked under the desk and the chair. He went to the filing cabinets and emptied out each and every file folder. He found nothing. He called one of the technicians in.

-Scan this room. Hit every corner with the friggin' Geiger counter.

The technician did as he was ordered and found no trace of radiation. Then, the Geiger counter gave off a crackle.

-Christ!

Before the Sergeant could react, the other technician called out from the hallway.

-Sgt. Rayno! Out here in the hallway. It's pretty strong.

Sgt. Rayno cursed himself.

-We should have turned the damned things on when we got off the elevator. Let's get out there.

The four men followed the Geiger counter's readings along the narrow hallway until-

-Man! The needle's skipping off the machine, Sergeant. You two better stay out here.

The two technicians went into the Men's room and let the Geiger counter do the searching. It didn't take long to find the piece. It was hidden in the cistern of the first stall.

-Here. Open the box and I'll take it out with the tongs.

Carefully, the technician dipped the metal tongs into the cistern and pulled out the segment and the timing device that was attached to it. He placed them into the lead container.

-Got it! Let's get the hell out of here.

They rejoined Sgt. Rayno and the police officer in the hallway.

-You got it?

-It's in here. It's just a fragment. It's affixed to some kind of timing device.

-Can we get the timer off of it?

-Too risky, Sgt. Rayno. We don't know what we're dealing with here. Let's get it downstairs and out of the building first.

Sgt. Rayno was forced to agree.

-Okay. Into the elevator, men. Hurry!

The four men started down and the timer did not go off, but something in the elevator triggered off the piece. It went off when the elevator car reached the 35th floor.

All four men were killed instantly along with every occupant on the five floors above and below. Other occupants in the building were either seriously injured by the initial explosion or poisoned by the intense radiation. The building's structural integrity remained intact.

Debris and glass rained down on to the street below. Pedestrians and police dodged the radioactive debris, but some were hit and injured.

The area around the building was cordoned off while the remaining occupants were evacuated along with the injured. The elevators were out of commission and the tenants had to be escorted down the one remaining stairwell in the dark. No electricity, the building's main generator was damaged. Ambulances arrived on the scene and more squad cars. Chaos was being replaced by order and a grimness that matched the catastrophe.

Louis Octavio was removed to St. Luke's isolation ward. He was a dying man. He was unconscious when taken out of the precinct house. His deal making days were over along with his murderous acts.

Dr. Claire Ingram was called in. Lt. Donovan and Edward were waiting for her to come out of the contamination unit. Finally, she emerged.

-He's dead.

Dr. Ingram was her usual brutally frank self.

-The body will have to be buried as radioactive waste. It's interesting though how his body's interior was so highly infected and yet the epidermis was relatively low level radiation. It's as if the internal organs soaked up the contamination like some sort of sponge which I know makes absolutely no sense.

Edward and Lt. Donovan were listening, but their thoughts strayed to their dead colleague, Sgt. Rayno. Neither man had spoken to each other about it nor to anyone else. Miss Raymond had quietly wept, but had not given voice to her feelings nor had Ginny Gray who was down at the crime scene and making a nuisance of herself.

Dr. Ingram continued.

-I'd like to see this "stone" or whatever it is. The radiation and its intensity and the inexplicable falling off could be applied to certain cancer treatments being worked on right now. It's not as far fetched as it sounds.

Neither Edward nor Lt. Donovan responded.

-Gentlemen? Just one last word. The radiation poisoning in Mr. Octavio suggested a sudden build-up. He wasn't sick for that long. He was only infected – and this is an educated guess –no more than a week ago – ten days, at most. Gentlemen?

Edward spoke up.

-I'm sorry, Doctor Ingram; but, we just lost a colleague and good friend. Sgt. Rayno was killed in that midtown blast.

Dr. Ingram took off her glasses.

-I'm sorry. Truly. Anyway, you may want to exhume those two men who were murdered in the Diamond District the other day. I'd like to do an autopsy on them.

Professor Moreland was having a cup of coffee with Miss Raymond at the 86th precinct house. The coffee was good because Miss Raymond had made it. The Professor had taken the initiative of visiting the precinct house after hearing of the midtown explosion.

-Cream and sugar, Professor?

-No. Thank you, Miss Raymond. I take it black.

-Here you go. Professor? You're sitting across from me, but your mind is someplace else. Whereabouts' is it, if I may ask?

He took a sip of the hot coffee.

-You're a perceptive young woman.

Miss Raymond waited for him to continue. When he did not, she picked up the slack

-It would have to be a problem of considerable consequence because the one we're tackling now is pretty intense. Professor, are you with me?

-I'm afraid, Miss Raymond, that my problem is theoretical for the time being.

-You mean that the problem doesn't exist yet? Is that what you're saying?

-It's on the perimeter of existence.

-It might help to get another opinion.

-You've enough on your plate as it is. They have re-
covered the bulk of the stone and the money, I take it.
I'm aware that Central Park was closed off.

Miss Raymond did her professional best not to react
to that last statement. This man knew too much.

-Is that what brings you here, Professor Moreland?

-What will happen with the stone that was recov-
ered today by Mr. Mendez? It's been shipped to the Aberdeen proving grounds?

Now, Miss Raymond had to ask her question.

-Who gave you that information?

-An educated guess. I worked with the military during the war. So, it is now in our possession.

Miss Raymond wasn't about to answer a disguised
inquiry. Let this man guess all he wanted to.

-I'm not following your line of reasoning, Professor
Moreland. Are you implying that the stone is better off
someplace else?

He put down his coffee.

-Not at all, Miss Raymond. The stone, at the present
time, doesn't concern me.   Perhaps, I'd better leave.
Good day.

Miss Raymond finished her coffee.

-Don't go. What does concern you?

-A woman by the name of Marlena Lake,

-I know of her.

-She is a pompous ass who had the gall to engage
me in my own office the other day. She asked the wrong
questions, Miss Raymond. Miss Lake wanted to know

about the Earth...she should have been asking about the satellite that orbits it.

Professor Moreland got up.

-I must go. Good day.

DECEMBER 4, 1948
FRIENDS FROM THE PAST

Seventeen

THE RADIATION count in the BMT subway tunnel had diminished to a safety level. The LL train that was destroyed could be removed along with the remaining corpses. At 500 5th Ave. the level of radiation that engulfed the surrounding floors was also beginning to level off. The building had been evacuated along with the adjoining buildings and the main branch of the public library across the street.

Edward Mendez was in his office and listening to the radio. The Mayor reopened the transit system both above ground and below with the exception of the LL line. Ridership had not been affected despite the ongoing fear and uncertainty. Fifth Ave. between 40th and 43rd St. was closed to traffic.

Edward turned off the radio and lit a cigarette. As far as anyone knew, one piece was still missing and could go off at any second. Every available cop was on duty and guarding the city. The undercover unit was searching every possible hiding place in all five boroughs which was a pretty daunting task considering the size and population of the city. Chances were that if it didn't go off, it might never be found.

Edward was doubtful about that last chance. It was meant to go off. What triggered the damned explosion...the timer...the vibration...what?

He took a deep drag on his cigarette. His mind kept coming back to his murdered sister. She was dead and the little there was in her diary was not helpful.

-Those two friends of hers: Linda Silverman and Rachel Schwartz. I think I'll track those two characters down. I can't just sit here on my backside.

He picked up the phone book and sorted through it for the two girls' surnames. He had no trouble finding them. He dialed Linda's number first.

-Hello?

-Edward Mendez calling. May I speak with Linda Silverman, please?

-This is she. Why are you calling?

Christ! She even sounds like Catrina, that same clipped manner of speaking.

-Miss Silverman? This is Catrina's brother, Edward. You knew my sister and that's the reason I'm calling. You may have information vital to a case I'm working on.

-How is that possible? I haven't spoken to your sister for quite some time.

Edward's patience was almost gone with this bitch.

-May I come over sometime today?

-Very well, Mr. Mendez. Six this evening and I can't spare you much time, so please be prompt.

-Thank you.

Edward slammed the phone down. He took a few drags on his cigarette to get his usually even keeled temper back. He dialed Rachel's number. It took a few rings for someone to answer.

-Hello?

-Hello. Edward Mendez calling. May I speak with Rachel Schwartz, please?

-Of course, I'll get her for you.

A human being!

-Hello? Is this Edward Mendez? I'm Rachel. I've read about you in the papers. You're Catrina's brother.

-Yes. I am. Rachel, I need to speak with you about a case I'm working on.

-Me? How exciting! What can I do to help?

-May I come over? I'd like to speak to you in person.

-Sure. What time?

-Say around six-thirty this evening if it's not interrupting your dinner.

-Heck no, Mr. Mendez. I'm the bohemian type. I keep real odd hours. See you around six-thirty.

How did Catrina ever become friends with such an affable person? He had a thought: he'd take Yolanda with him. It might be a little intimidating for those two ladies to face him on their own. Having a woman with him would soften the effect.

Eighteen

EDWARD SPENT the rest of the morning and early afternoon catching up on paper work, going to the barber's downstairs for a haircut and getting his shoes polished.

He was in his car heading uptown to the ice rink to pick up Yolanda. He was driving by 14th St. when he noticed a '31 Buick turn the corner behind him. But, his thoughts at the moment were about Sgt. Rayno. His ice hockey friend was dead. The one person at the 86th St. precinct he trusted. They had tickets for tonight's Rangers game at Madison Square Garden. Edward still had the tickets in his coat pocket.

The P. I. pulled up to the ice rink and waited for Yolanda. The '31 Buick drove by but Edward barely noticed it.

Yolanda came out of the front entrance with her duffel bag and after a welcoming kiss and embrace, the couple headed out to Brooklyn.

-So, you want me along to soften that masculine blow?

-You're perceptive, baby, and you've got that feminine insight. This Linda chick sounded as cold as the North Pole.

-And, you want me to chip away at the ice?

-Something like that. You'll know what to do when we get there. Just play it by ear.

-And, this other woman...Rachel? You know, Edward, they won't be so young anymore.

The P. I. laughed. He turned on the car's windshield wipers. A light snow was beginning to fall.

-I hadn't thought of that. You see? We haven't even gotten there and you're already two steps ahead of me.

-So, what about Rachel? Was she nicer than ice cold Linda?

-By a couple of football fields. Said she was the bohemian type.

-Edward, you know, they're thinking about declaring Marshall Law. I just heard it on the radio before I left the rink.

-I'll be damned. But, I can understand why. You know, baby, I've got one problem with this: if Octavio didn't plant this hypothetical third bomb, then it must have been one of the goons in the gray van.

-What about that woman, Eileen Kobe, the one Octavio killed?

-Maybe.

-But, you don't think so.

-I don't. From the little we know of her, she just doesn't fit the pattern.

-So, why are we seeing these two women?

-Because, my sister had to confide in someone. I'm counting on that.

They crossed over the Brooklyn Bridge and headed toward Borum Hill which wasn't that far from the Mendez home. Edward found a parking space easily enough.

-Well, here goes nothing.

Yolanda looked at her wristwatch.

-It's almost six o'clock, so we're on time. She said that she couldn't spare you much time.

Edward turned off the windshield wipers.

-Which is probably a blessing in disguise. Let's head on in.

The door was opened by Linda Silverman. She was a petite and thin woman who was well "coiffed" as Edward's sister Victoria would phrase it. She showed them into an over decorated living room.

-Linda? I know that you can't spare much time.

-I stated that over the phone.

-Yes. You did. I'll get straight to the point. My sister was murdered two days ago. She was beaten to death.

No reaction.

-Go on.

-Yes. Did she ever confide in you-

-We had many confidences which I will not betray.

Edward took out a cigarette, but didn't light up.

-You may have to. I came here on a matter of life and death. Did she ever – and please don't interrupt – mention a Mr. Louis Octavio or a Mr. Ricardo Montenegro? This concerns the recent bombings in the city.

Edward and Yolanda waited for an answer. Yolanda could see that the woman sitting opposite her had had a face-lift recently. It hardened her look and even accentuated the tiny lines around the woman's eyes.

-I don't know how I can help you. Your sister and I have not been in contact for years.

-Did you part friends?

Yolanda asked that question and it took Linda by surprise.

-Why do you ask?

Yolanda smiled coyly at this acerbic woman.

-You haven't answered my question, Miss Silverman.

-The name Octavio was mentioned...but I don't remember the context.

Edward leaned forward.

-I think you do, lady.

-Are you calling me a liar, Mr. Mendez?

-What did Catrina say about Mr. Octavio?

-I don't recall.

Liar! Edward tried a different tact.

-Did Catrina ever give you anything? A keepsake or present?

-We never exchanged presents.

-Never? I don't believe you. Don't hold out on me, Miss Silverman. If I have to, I'll bring the police with me next time and that's not an idle threat.

Linda got up.

-I've answered your questions. And, now I must ask you to leave.

Edward knew it would be useless to press her. He and Yolanda left.

Back in the Ford.

-Edward, she was lying. Did you notice how her eyes kept darting to the upstairs part of the house?

-Now that you mention it, I did. Whatever Catrina gave her has to be someplace on the second floor.

-So, how will you get it?

-Lt. Donovan can get a search warrant and maybe that will put the fear of God in that bitch.

He started up the car.

-Let's head over to Rachel's place. It's only a few blocks from here.

-Why not leave the car here? We can walk and you won't have to look around for another parking space. It's stopped snowing.

Edward patted her on the cheek.

-You're on. I could use the exercise.

In a few minutes, they were standing in front of Rachel's three story brownstone. Every floor was alive with the sound of people and music.

-Sounds like Rachel is having a party. I can hear the music from out here.

-A real contrast to Linda's place, that's for damned sure,.

Edward knocked on the door. They waited for a couple of minutes before a middle-aged woman answered. She had on a loose fitting blouse and bohemian pants. Her hair was a little too long and she wore no make-up.

-I'll bet you're Edward Mendez. And, you're Yolanda Estravades, the ice skater. Oh, I've seen your picture in the papers. Come on in!

Rachel practically shoved them into a small dining room just off the main hallway.

-Have a seat. Nobody will bother us in here. I don't serve any food at my parties...just booze and plenty of it. Can I offer you a drink? A friend brought over some fancy bourbon.

Edward and Yolanda declined the offer.

-Suit yourselves. Now, how can I help you?

Edward wanted to hug this wonderful woman. Yolanda liked her, too, but thought she was a little too friendly.

-Rachel, my sister, Catrina, was murdered.

-Oh, God! How awful! I'm so sorry to hear it. When did it happen? Why? Oh, Mr. Mendez...I'm rambling on. I mean...me and Catrina didn't really part as friends...but to be murdered... Are you going to solve the case?

-In a manner of speaking, Rachel. But, I have to ask you this: did Catrina ever mention anyone to you by the name of Louis Octavio or Ricardo Montenegro?

-No...not that I remember. We never talked much about boys. You know, come to think of it, I don't think she or Linda had any boyfriends. That's where I didn't fit in. I've always been boy crazy myself. Those two were always talking about clothes and jewelry and taking holidays...and always to Mexico! Why Mexico? What the hell was so special about Mexico? And, to get back to Linda, I don't think she ever married. She takes care of her elderly mom, you know. I guess it gives her something to do. Oh, God! I sound so catty.

Edward didn't know about Linda's mother.

-Rachel, did Catrina ever give you anything in the way of presents?

-Who? Me? Forget it! Catrina wasn't generous that way. I'm not really helping much, am I?

Edward smiled in bemusement.

-Rachel, how did you and my sister ever become friends?

-Good question! I'm not too sure, you know. Just one day she started chatting me up and invited me to come along with her and Linda to her house. I almost turned her down. But, for some reason, she wanted me along. I've never figured it out.

Edward didn't know what to say. He didn't want to offend this woman because he thought he just hit upon the reason.

Rachel rambled on.

-But, it's kind of interesting...well, sort of...my ex-husband actually ran into Catrina last year...right before the sun did a disappearing act. She just got back from one of her holidays, I guess. He knew her from high school, like me, but really didn't like her. No offense.

-None taken.

-They were civil to each other; but, she said something odd.

Edward was alert to the extreme.

-Like what?

-Well, my ex-husband, Charlie, he's here as a matter of fact, if you want to talk to him. He brought over most of the booze.

-You tell me first, Rachel.

-She said, Catrina, that is, that she had seen Linda and that the meeting was a fruitful one. Your sister would say something like that. Charlie didn't say anything. He really didn't know how to react. He never liked Linda either. That's the reason I broke off with them, because of Charlie.

-Just how "fruitful" was this meeting?

-She, Catrina, that is, gave Linda a special lipstick from Mexico. Again! Mexico! Was your sister obsessed with that place?

Edward tried not to laugh, but wasn't too successful.

-What kind of a lipstick?

-She didn't say because Charlie asked her – he's the curious type, like me -- and of course Miss Catrina had to be mysterious and a snob. Oh, I'm sorry.

-Don't be. You knew my sister to the proverbial "T." Rachel, thanks a lot and try to stay indoors for the next couple of day. Savvy?

-Sure. Now, can I get you and Yolanda here a drink?

Nineteen

WHEN THEY got back to the car, the P. I. opened up the trunk and got out his Geiger counter.

-You can stay in the car, if you want, baby.

-Are you kidding? Stay out here all alone? I'm coming with you. And, besides, I can help with her elderly mother.

-Let's go, then.

For the second time that night, Edward knocked hard on Linda Silverman's front door.

-Where the hell is she? She can't have gone to bed already.

-Try, again, Edward. She probably knows it's us and doesn't want to answer.

The P. I. rapped on the door even harder. They heard footsteps from inside the house.

-Someone's coming.

A voice from inside replied.

-Who is there, please?

Yolanda whispered.

-Edward, it must be Linda's mother. Let me talk. Mrs. Silverman, my mane is Yolanda Estravades and Mr. Edward Mendez is here also. Please. We must talk with your daughter. Would you be so kind as to let us in?

The door was opened by an elderly woman with a pink, woolen shawl wrapped around her shoulders. She looked frightened, but otherwise composed.

-Come in. It's such a cold night. Let's go into the parlor where it's warm.

Yolanda took the woman by the elbow and helped her.

-Mrs. Silverman, where is Linda?

-I honestly don't know, Miss Estravades. She left me all alone.

Edward spoke to her.

-Mrs. Silverman, may I look about your house? I won't touch anything. It really is urgent.

The old lady cast him a shrewd glance.

-That's a Geiger counter you've got there, isn't it? Yes. Of course. Please, go ahead with your search, Mr. Mendez. It'll be a relief to know that my house isn't radioactive.

-I'll stay with her, Edward.

The P. I. scanned the house from top to bottom and found no trace of radioactivity except for some residual readings in Linda's bedroom from her vanity dresser.

Edward rejoined the two women in the living room.

-Mrs. Silverman, did your daughter take anything with her when she left the house this evening?

-Only her handbag and, of course, her hat and coat. Has it stopped snowing? Such dreadful weather we're having, lately...ever since the sun disappeared last year.

Edward waited for Mrs. Silverman to finish her musings. Inadvertently, she reminded him of something that he kept forgetting to ask Marlena. He continued his questions.

-Any idea where Linda might have gone?

-None at all.

-Did she ever mention getting a gift from my sister, Catrina Mendez?

-Yes. She did. A rather gaudy looking lipstick case. It wasn't very pretty. I don't mean to sound ungracious.

-May I use your phone?

-Of course.

The old woman turned to Yolanda.

-What has my headstrong daughter done? I'm not blind to her faults so you needn't be kind.

-We don't know that she's done anything, Mrs. Silverman.

Edward placed his phone call to the Park Slope police precinct. It was brief and to the point. He hung up and turned to Mrs. Silverman.

-I don't want to alarm you, Mrs. Silverman, but I'm about to have the police put out an APB for your daughter.

-I think I understand. It's for withholding information or possibly for something even worse.

-I'll be frank with you. Yes. And, Mrs. Silverman, what's your daughter's means of support?

-As far as I know, she draws from a fund.

-From what bank?

-From the Hamburg Savings and Loan bank. She doesn't think that I know, but I do.

-Who set up this fund?

Mrs. Silverman smiled.

-My daughter's not unattractive. I believe a male friend.

-But- never mind. Did you ever meet him?

-Never set eyes on him . Don't even know his name. I believe...well, I'll just come right out and say it. She and your sister spoke of a certain man who had a Latin sounding name...Octavio, I think..

-May I use your phone, again?

-Make as many phone call as you need to, Mr. Mendez. I'll help all I can even if my daughter won't.

And, aside to Yolanda.

-Never liked that Catrina. Always looked down her nose at everyone as if she were something special. She wasn't and you can take my word for it.

Edward placed his call to Lt. Donovan.

-Hello? Lieutenant Donovan? Edward Mendez here. Listen, I've got a heads up on that bomb. The Park Slope police should be on their way to Linda Silverman's place just about now. The piece was put in a lipstick case. I know. I know! Linda Silverman...she's a walking keg of radioactive dynamite who just might blow up half of Brooklyn.

Edward turned to Mrs. Silverman.

-Do you have a photo of your daughter?

-Yes. I'll get it for you.

Yolanda got up.

-Just tell me where to find it. I'll go.

-Thank you, young lady. It's upstairs on my dresser bureau. It was taken before her face-lift, but it still looks like her.

Yolanda walked over to Edward.

-I'll be right back.

-Lieutenant? You still there?

-I'm still here, Mendez. As soon as I get off the phone, I'll put out an APB of my own just to stir things up.

-Good. 'Cause that chick is up to something and it's not good.

DECEMBER 5, 1948
MANHUNT

Twenty

-WITHOLDING EVIDENCE is a crime. And, if this woman is holding out on us, I'll have her sent up for life. What the hell is she on the run for?

It was past midnight and everyone in that Interrogation Room was tired both physically and mentally. The absence of Sgt. Rayno was acutely felt. Everyone in the station house liked the Sergeant.

Lt. Donovan continued.

-And, her mother and this Rachel Schwartz woman have no idea where she might have gone?

Edward put out his second cigarette.

-Linda is the anti-social type. No friends that anyone knows of and no living relatives except for her mother.

-How about enemies, Mendez? Everybody has those.

Edward tried laughing.

-We just don't know. And, that fund she's been living off of? It's under the name of Romo-Ark, Inc.

Lt. Donovan raised an eyebrow.

-The metal and ore company? What the hell do they call it...tool and dye...something like that. I hear they're also developing computer systems and missile launchers. They're all over the god-damned place.

Edward nodded.

-That's the one.

-But, who initiated this fund? Who okay-ed it? We need a name, damn it!

Miss Raymond spoke waving cigarette smoke away from her face.

-We're looking into it, Lieutenant. But, that company is vast. It's global. Our boys are having trouble sifting through the bureaucratic barriers.

Edward lit his cigarette.

-Edward?

-What is it, baby?

-How many cigarettes does that make?

-I'll make this one last. Just had a thought. It's wild, but what the hell?

He had everyone's attention.

-Just maybe Linda's gone to someone at Romo-Ark. It makes sense. She gets her money from them, so she must have a contact. Or...I just had another thought. You see, baby, smoking helps. What about those gray vans that keep popping up? Octavio was connected to them, somehow. And, if I'm not mistaken, so was my sister. But, for sure, check out Romo-Ark's top executives, Miss Raymond.

-We are, Eddie. We're going through their Accounting Dept. right now. That corporation is never closed for business.

Yolanda bristled at Miss Raymond's familiarity with her boyfriend.

Lt. Donovan put out a cigarette.

-We checked out that gray van. Its license plates were phony – no big surprise – and its driver and two passengers are being looked over by the medics. The preliminary results, which I've got right here, says they were normal enough, but their bodies were lacking iron and bordering on anemic. Doesn't really help us much, but there it is. And, one more thing: we're putting Linda Silverman's photo on the front page of every city newspaper. Like it or not, she's gonna' be a celebrity.

-Oh? Do you think she's still in the city?

-Yes, Miss Estravades, I do. Just call it a cop's gut feeling.

Yolanda continued.

-You know, I still think she's afraid of someone. She kept staring up at the ceiling and...

Lt. Donovan prodded her.

-Go on.

-And, there was only her mother in the house.

Edward finished her thought.

-And her mother didn't look too much like an invalid. A little frail, maybe, but well enough.

Edward reached for his pack of cigarettes.

-But, why pay Linda *any* money? Why not just bump her off? It's got to be that she sold them something awfully valuable and part of the agreement was for her to keep quiet about it.

-Like what? A piece of the stone? But, she's been on their payroll for years.

-I've been thinking that one over. Linda Silverman and my sister sold Romo-Ark one of the two stones. They were paid off: my sister probably got one big lump sum for it and Linda opted for a lifetime allowance. Then, my sister got greedy and had no trouble persuading Linda to sell the second stone to Octavio.

Yolanda could believe that last part.

-Why would your sister split the profit? She didn't strike me as the generous type.

-Well, baby, she needed what we call a go-between. She never ventured beyond her own known sphere.

Lt. Donovan's laugh was nasty.

-I'd like to raise your sister from the god-damned dead and ask her a few pointed questions. And, then, I'd throw her back in her coffin and pour salt in the grave.

Edward didn't want to laugh, but he did in spite of himself.

Yolanda asked a question.

-But, what does Romo-Ark *do* with it? It's pretty dangerous stuff.

-Professor Moreland could probably answer that better than any of us, baby. Maybe, they could use it for some kind of rocket fuel or alternate source of energy.

They've got the resources and the money to experiment with it. Marlena suggested it could be used constructively.

Lt. Donovan agreed.

-In that case, Miss Silverman's probably run off to Romo-Ark to get rid of what she had left in the lipstick holder. She was holding out on them. Maybe, she wanted an increase in her allowance. If so, she's playing with some pretty ruthless people.

Edward agreed with the Lieutenant.

-I might have scared her off. I hope you're right, Lieutenant because if she's sold that piece to Romo-Ark chances are good they won't misuse it. It'd be too valuable to them. As a matter of fact, they'd have the world market cornered.

-But, we can't make that assumption. We've gotta' go with the fact that Linda's at large and dangerous. We've got a squad car outside her house in Borum Hill on the out chance that she returns home. And, we've got men posted at the HQ of Romo-Ark right here in the city.

Yolanda asked her question as she inhaled the smoke from her boyfriend's cigarette.

-Do you think she might be home? That maybe she never left?

Lt. Donovan responded.

-I doubt it. We've been through the house a couple of times with a fine tooth comb and found nothing and no one except her mother.

Yolanda continued her line of inquiry.

-What about Rachel's place? Might be a good place to hide with so many people going in and out all the time. I know they weren't girlfriends anymore, but Rachel would be the sort who would help her.

-Your girlfriend makes a good point, Mendez. I'll get a squad car over there...pronto!

Edward and Yolanda were driving home. There was virtually no traffic at this early hour of the morning.

-Edward?

-I see him. That same Buick that's been tailing us since we left the precinct.

-At least it's not one of those gray vans. And, I don't see anyone in the car except the driver. And, I can't really make out his face. It's too dark and the street lights don't help.

-Don't look back any more. When we reach your place, I'll make it so that he's gotta' pass us by. Try and get a glimpse of him then. And, do you notice that I haven't asked for a cigarette?

-Good boy. And, we're almost at our apartment.

-I'm going to pull over so get ready to look.

Edward pulled the car over to park and the Buick passed them by.

-Did you get a good look at him, baby?

-An older man with gray hair and a goatee, but no mustache. He looked over at us as he went by. I got the impression that he was about your height and built.

-And?

-He sort of looked familiar. Maybe, I passed him on the street or saw his picture in the papers.

-Good work. I wonder what he wants?

-You mean: what is he up to?

DECEMBER 6, 1948
NOR'EASTER

Twenty-one

EDWARD WAS lying in bed next to Yolanda. He was staring up at the ceiling, but not really seeing it. The manhunt for Linda Silverman was entering its second day. She was an inexperienced criminal, technically speaking, but New York City offered a lot of hiding places.

Edward reached for the phone, but stopped himself. It was only 5:00 A.M. What of it? He dialed Mrs. Silverman's number. The phone was picked up on the second ring.

-Hello?

-Mrs. Silverman? Edward Mendez. I hope I didn't wake you up.

-You didn't, Mr. Mendez. I really couldn't sleep. I've been more or less pacing the floor and drinking tea which I don't even like.

-I'm not a tea drinker either. Mrs. Silverman? Do you know where your daughter is?

-Haven't a clue, Mr. Mendez. And, I've been thinking about it a great deal. Her only friend was your sister. And, she's dead.

Edward sat up in bed.

-Mrs. Silverman, did the two of them exchange letters?

-Yes and no. Linda wrote letters to your sister when
she traveled. Catrina sent only postcards, mostly from
Mexico and sometimes from London. It seemed that she
never went anywhere else. And, yes, I read the postcards: perfunctory and boring.

-That sounds like my sister, all right.

-She filled Linda's head with ideas. I don't mean to
sound disrespectful, but there it is.

-Why didn't Linda travel with her.

-That's a question that I often asked my daughter.
Of course, she would always blame me: her invalid
mother. Mr. Mendez, I am no invalid and perfectly ca-
pable of taking care of myself. Granted, I have a house-
keeper come in twice a week for the heavy cleaning and
to do grocery shopping.

-And, Linda had no other friends?

-Just that oddball, Rachel; but, they were more ac-
quaintances than friends.

-Did Linda go out much?

-Not very often. Always staring out the window like
some young girl waiting for her boyfriend to show up.
She would go for a walk in the park now and then, but
not for very long.

-Did she ever meet anyone there?

-I don't think so. She wasn't at all the friendly type. And, I would tell her, Mr. Mendez, to take a trip to Mexico and join your sister. Although, I'll never understand the attraction to that country. Goodness! You can't even drink the water. Dreadful place, in my opinion. I do suspect that Linda might have gone outside to place phone calls to that company, Romo-Ark. She never actually worked for them, you know. She never worked a day in her life.

-How did she come by that fund of hers?

-I wish I knew. And, not that I haven't tried to find out. But...well, on Linda's "outings" I did sneak a peek at some of her correspondence and one name kept popping up: a Mr. Richard Aster.

Yolanda was almost ready to leave. Edward was lighting his second cigarette when the phone rang. The two of them started and stared at the phone.

-I'd better answer answer it.

Edward motioned for her to do just that.

-Hello?

-Put Edward Mendez on. I know he's there.

Yolanda recognized the clipped voice with the accusatory tone.

-Hold on, please.

She put her hand over the mouthpiece.

-Edward! It's Linda Silverman. I'm sure of it. How did she get this number? It's not listed in the directory.

He took the phone.

-Edward Mendez.

-This is Linda Silverman. You've been looking for me. I see that I've made the front page of today's New York Times.

-And, every other newspaper. Miss Silverman? Turn yourself in. Or, if you prefer, I'll come for you.

-You will both come for me.

-What do you mean by that?

Edward didn't like the edge to this woman's voice.

-You and your ice skater girlfriend.

-Leave my girlfriend out of this, lady. I mean it.

-Edward what is she saying? I want to know.

-Miss Silverman, stop this game playing. It's a pretty deadly game. Now, please, where are you calling from?

-You and Miss Estravades will meet me at the Myrtle Ave. and Broadway transfer point. It was the route that Mr. Octavio used for his escape.

-You know that? How?

-I will be waiting on the train platform near where the conductor operates the doors. The time will be 10 A.M. You have approximately four hours to plan your double-cross.

-Will you bring the segment with you, Miss Silverman?

-I will be waiting for you. Don't be late. And, Mr. Mendez? If any attempt is made to apprehend me, I will detonate the piece of stone at that rather busy terminal.

-Miss Silverman? Hello? She hung up.

Edward slammed the phone down. He related his instructions to Yolanda.

-Why is she doing this, Edward? What does she want?

He thought about it for a second.

-Her voice sounded more clipped than ever – like some god-damned robot giving a programmed speech.

-Then, someone must be giving her orders.

-Sounds like it. I've gotta call Donovan. Man, is he gonna' love this.

Yolanda canceled her training session and was now sitting with Edward in the Interrogation Room at the 86th St. precinct. Lt. Donovan, Miss Raymond and two other police officers were there as well. The time was 6:45 A.M.

-Okay, Mendez, was there any background noise that you could hear from where this woman was calling?

-Some passing traffic, but no voices.

-I'd like to know who's been helping her 'cause for someone anti-social, she's done all right for herself. Anyway, we're gonna' have squad cars tailing every train on that elevated line, from Myrtle Ave. right down to Marcy Ave. at the Williamsburg Bridge. And, they'll be undercover men on that platform. Don't worry, we'll get her.

-How about on the train me and Yolanda will be riding?

Lt. Donovan reached for a cigarette, but his pack was empty.

-They'll be two men in your car. And...why the hell can't she just turn it in? She hasn't broken any laws for Christ's sake...but she's coming mighty close...*mighty* close. 'Cause if this dame's got that segment on her, she's endangering innocent people. And, I will throw the god-damned book at her.

Miss Raymond spoke.

-Eddie? Yolanda? We'll have you covered every inch of the way. On the train and on the ground. And, by the way, we've come up with a name for these pieces: trigger stones. Not very original, I'm afraid.

Edward offered the Lieutenant a Lucky Strike.

-I'd like to know what exactly triggers them off?

Miss Raymond hazarded a guess.

-Lieutenant, we're assuming the detonation device..like plastic explosives.

Edward put his own theory out.

-Maybe. But, when you think about it, the first trigger stone went off in a subway tunnel underwater. The second one went off descending in an elevator at a pretty high altitude. So, just maybe, it's a change in pressure...atmospheric pressure that sets them off.

Everyone in the room agreed with his theory.

Edward continued.

-I heard on the radio this morning that there's a nor'easter headed for the city – like we need more lousy weather. As a matter of fact, it should hit pretty soon. That would change the atmospheric pressure, especially over water – like a train crossing over a bridge from Brooklyn into Manhattan.

Lt. Donovan nodded gravely.

-Then, we've gotta' grab that trigger stone before the train starts over the bridge.

Twenty-two

IT WAS 9:00 A.M. when Edward and Yolanda boarded the QJ train at 168th St. in Jamaica, Queens. The train wasn't crowded so the P. I. and his girlfriend got the seats they wanted: seats facing in a horizontal direction...in the direction of the train. The conductor closed the doors and they were on their way to the agreed upon rendezvous point. There were undercover men in the car and Edward thought he spotted two of them: one at each end of the car.

Yolanda turned to her boyfriend with a worried look on her pretty face.

-Edward, I just had a terrible thought.

-Like what, baby?

He took out a cigarette, but didn't light it.

-Suppose there's a delay of some kind, like signal problems or a sick passenger? It could happen.

-Any signal problem is going to have to be ignored. And, as far as a sick passenger? He'll have to be hauled off the train and taken to a token booth clerk. This train can't be stopped for anything.

The train traveled at an even clip and made the usual stops. More passengers were getting on at each stop than were getting off. Pretty soon there were people standing and holding on to leather straps.

After half an hour, when they pulled out of Broadway Junction, Edward and Yolanda grew tense. Up until then, they had about twenty stops between them and the current station.

Edward squeezed Yolanda's hand.

-Baby, there are too many people on this train. It's going to make it plenty awkward.

-I was just thinking that. That undercover cop is still over there. He's standing up now. I guess so that we can see him.

Edward took a glance at the back of the car.

-The other one's still there, too. Maybe, we should try and get some of these commuters into another car or off the damned train altogether.

Yolanda grabbed him by the shoulder.

-Don't do that. It would cause a panic, for sure, and that would probably delay the train.

-I thought it was past the damned rush hour.

-Some of these people are holiday shoppers. And, keep your voice down! Look. Only two more stops to go. We're almost there. I think we're a little early.

-Yolanda, we'd better get near an exit door. It'll open up on the right side of the car.

-Does she want us to step off the train?

-I don't know. I don't think so. What worries me is that she's not asking for anything except us. Look. We just pulled into Kosciusko St. One more stop to go. Let's get up and position ourselves by the door. Come on.

-Edward, it's starting to hail. I can hear the pellets hitting the window.

The two of them got up and their seats were immediately taken up by two other passengers. They had to push their way past the standing commuters until they made it to one of the the exit doors.

Edward was tempted to light the cigarette that he'd been holding on to for the better part of an hour now; but, he knew it was against Transit rules.

-We're pulling into the station, baby. This train's moving too fast, so I can't really make out faces in the crowd. But, we're slowing down, I think. Yes! Baby, she's standing there!

-Where? Yes. I see her now. That's her just standing there without even a hat on..

The train came to a stop. A few passengers got off, but even more got on. It was slippery on the wooden platform and commuters had to tread carefully. A few slipped, but no one fell.

Linda Silverman spotted Edward and Yolanda standing by the open door. Edward was hoping she'd slip so he could get her off guard; but, she held her balance as she got on to the waiting train a door further down but in the same car.

-Edward, now what?

-Let's walk over to her.

The train pulled out of the station. They made their way to Linda Silverman who was standing near an undercover cop.

-Stop right there, Mr. Mendez.

A few of the nearby commuters turned to stare.

-Linda? We're here as you asked.

-As I demanded.

-Have it your way, lady. So, now what? What is it that you want? Do you have the segment with you?

-So many questions.

-Just answer one, if you would. And, don't play footsy with me.

-Yes. I have the piece in the lipstick case...so heavy; but, I imagine anything made of lead would be heavy.

The train pulled into Flushing Ave. There were three more to go before it reached the Williamsburg Bridge.

-Are you willing to hand it over?

-Another question, Mr. Mendez? Let me tell you a few things that I think you should know.

-We're listening.

-There were two stones given to your father who in turn gave them to his wife to hold for his son. You were an infant when Manuel Mendez died. Your mother hid the stones in a lead lined compartment in the cellar of your house.

-Tell me what I don't know.

-Don't interrupt me!

Yolanda grabbed Edward's arm and whispered to him.

-Edward, let her talk. Look at her eyes...looks like she's in some kind of trance.

Linda Silverman continued with her story.

-Catrina confided all this to me because it was a burden she couldn't bear by herself. I eased that burden for her.

The train pulled into Lorimer Ave.

-It was I who persuaded your sister to sell one of the stones for a more than reasonable sum of money. We could keep the second stone for a rainy day, so to speak. I knew of Romo-Ark, Mr. Mendez. I knew they would pay generously for such merchandise. I did my research. Catrina was more than willing to take one...yes...steal it and sell it. We'd be set for life. The idea was entirely mine. Your sister didn't have the imagination to come up with such a daring plan. I did.

The train pulled into Hewes Ave.

-Who was your contact at Romo-Ark?

-That, I will not tell you.

-Did my mother know about any of this?

-No. Catrina didn't dare tell her. Your mother would have disowned her for violating your father's trust. But, your sister was greedy. Maybe I was, too. But, then her accident occurred during that séance you held. She wanted more money to heal her scars. She planned on going to Brazil for some kind of operation. A fool's errand that would have been.

-So, that's why she sold the remaining stone to Octavio.

-Yes. She was a fool to trust such a man. And, it was he who gave me this "piece" of merchandise.

-How did she come to know Octavio?

-Through your father's rather infamous lodge, of course. Octavio had an underling working for him.

-Linda, what do *you* want?

The train pulled into Marcy Ave. When it was ready to pull out it would cross over the Williamsburg Bridge. The pressure in the atmosphere was dropping rapidly.

-Can't you guess, Mr. Mendez? Perhaps, you can't. I want the remaining pieces that the police took from Octavio in Central Park.

-How do you know about that? None of those details were in any of the papers.

-Suffice it to say that I know all the salient details.

-Are you serious, lady?

-Yes. I am.

-Where's your segment?

-In my purse in the rather tasteless lipstick container your sister gave to me. Don't move toward me or I'll trigger it off.

-So, you give us a piece in exchange for nearly an entire stone that could level half the planet? That's one rotten deal, lady. What if I don't go for it?

The woman sitting down behind Linda and next to the undercover cop caught the full impact of that last sentence and screamed.

-She's got a bomb! Oh, my God! The woman's got a bomb! Run for your life!

It was enough to set off a panic in the train car. Everyone sitting down got to their feet and the shoving began. People headed to the connecting door at the opposite end of the car to get out.

The train started to cross the bridge. Edward grabbed a hold of Linda Silverman by the waist. The undercover cop snatched her bag.

-Here! Take her! Let me have the bag.

The undercover cop threw Edward the bag and cuffed Linda Silverman.

Edward opened up the connecting door and straddled the two cars He got ready to toss the bag into the river. Yolanda stood in the open doorway and screamed.

-Edward, behind you – look out!

He'd been facing Yolanda and now turned to see a black suited man aiming a gun at him. But, first things first and with one powerful swing, the P. I. tossed the bag into the river below.

The black suited man cried out.

-No!

-Too bad, pal.

Edward caught the man by the arm just as the piece exploded in mid-air. The shock wave hit the train swinging it from side to side. People were tossed to the floor and Edward almost fell between the two cars to his death. He braced his arms on the metal pinions and kicked the black suited man full in the stomach. The man lost his balance and fell into the white radioactive cloud below. Yolanda and the undercover cop pulled Edward back into the car.

-Edward, are you all right?

-I think so, baby. That was a close one.

-Your hands...

-That's from hanging on by my finger nails. Man! That guy almost pulled me over with him.

Edward addressed the undercover cop.

-Hey, guy? Thanks for the assist. We'd better get transit to shut down this line for awhile.

The train crossed over the bridge and entered the subway tunnel.

-As soon as we pull into Delancey St., we'll get right on it, Mr. Mendez. But, that radiation....it was kind of hovering over the water like some friggin' cloud of death.

-It oughta' stay hovering right where it is unless this storm pushed it down into the water. The Coast Guard better stop any river traffic for a while or at least divert it.

Yolanda, still holding on to him, asked.

-Edward, is the danger past?

-For now, baby. We'll have a patrol car pick us up. Lt. Donovan's going to want a briefing.

-Edward? Look at Linda.

Linda Silverman was standing stock still in handcuffs. She was staring straight ahead, but her eyes weren't seeing anything.

And, at the 86th St. precinct on the third floor Interrogation Room...

-So, one of those goons was on the train with you?

-I'll say!

Lt. Donovan opened a fresh pack of cigarettes.

-Then, there *is* a definite connection between Romo-Ark and those gray vans.

-Sure looks like it.

-So, are all the segments and fragments of segments accounted for? Say yes. Is the city- the world out of danger?

-My P. I. gut instinct says yes, Lieutenant. We've got three quarters and a few splinters of one stone and Romo-Ark has the other stone.

-And, Mendez? You look kinda' puzzled about something. Give.

-Octavio was working for Romo-Ark. Why give up the stone fragments at Central Park? Makes no friggin' sense. Why not just keep them or sell them off to the highest bidder? Why would Romo-Ark let them go?

-I've been wondering about that myself. It's like they wanted us to have the segments.

Yolanda was incredulous.

-To blow ourselves up?

-Yes. Miss Estravades. I think you just might be right about that. Or maybe our own government is connected with Romo-Ark in some way.

Not that he cared, but Edward had to ask.

-What about Linda Silverman? Did you get anything out of her?

Lt. Donovan lit up.

-That's kind of tough. The chick slipped into a catatonic state. They've got her up at Bellevue for observation.

-Catatonic state? What the hell is the prognosis?

-Don't know. Why, Mendez? You look kind of lost yourself.

-It's just that when you said "catatonic" it rang a bell somewhere in the back of my head. But never mind that. What's the latest on Ricardo Montenegro?

-We're still on to that case. He might turn up. We're hoping that he does.

Edward shook his head.

-Not likely.

Yolanda smiled at Lt. Donovan.

-Now what, Lieutenant?

-Well, Miss Estravades- Yolanda, the case is officially closed. The city's functioning on all cylinders except for the subway tunnel on the BMT line which had to be shut down for repairs.

Edward lit a much needed cigarette...and a moment of apprehension seized him as he exhaled a cloud of smoke.

EPILOGUE

-MOTHER, WHAT do you make of this article?

-Which one, dear? You know that I have varied interests.

-This one about an unmanned rocket to orbit the moon.

-Yes. Exploring the infinite frontier of space. I approve.

-I wonder if they'll find anything interesting.

-I'm certain they will. Perhaps, something even more interesting than they expect.

Susan cast her mother a significant look.

-What exactly do you mean by that?

-I'm merely hypothesizing, but theories do abound.

-Name me one, please.

-That before life began on this planet, an advanced civilization thrived on the moon.

-Do you believe it's actually true and worth the expense of a research rocket?

-Of course. It's quite thrilling, the prospect...and, perhaps, dangerous.

-Why dangerous?

-There is always danger in the "unknown."

-Mother, to change the subject, there's been a blue Buick parked outside our house for several days now. It moves only when it has to avoid being ticketed. I saw an elderly man get out of that car just once. You know who he is, don't you?

-Yes. And, you're a very observant girl. Good. I've trained you well

-Well, who is he? You're not going to hold out on me, are you? Oh God! I sound like Edward.

Marlena took a puff on her just lit cigar.

-Manuel Mendez: Edward's father.

Next

Romo-Ark

AN EDWARD MENDEZ, P. I. THRILLER

BOOK VI

About the Author

GERARD DENZA has worked in the Publicity Dept. at Random House and Little, Brown, and Company in New York City. He's worked with such authors as Kevin and Todd Berger, Pete Hamill, Willie Morris and Arthur C. Clarke.

He's also the playwright and director of six Off-Off Broadway plays which include: ICARUS, MAHLER: THE MAN WHO WAS NEVER BORN, THE DYING GOD: A VAMPIRE'S TALE, SHADOWS BEHIND THE FOOTLIGHTS and THE HOUSEDRESS. His noir play, EDMUND: THE LIKELY, has been recorded for radio broadcast.

Mr. Denza is a graduate of Fordham University at Lincoln Center where he majored in psychology and graduated with honors: Magna Cum Laude. He lives in New York City and is hard at work on his next novel.

Made in the USA
Middletown, DE
08 February 2021